I0445269

Getting Ghosted Too

Amelia Dax

© 2025 Amelia Dax
All rights reserved

This is a work of fiction. Names, characters, places, and incidents either are the products of the author's imagination or used fictitiously. Any resemblance to actual persons, living or dead, businesses, companies, events, or locales is entirely coincidental.

No part of this book may be reproduced, or stored in a retrieval system, or transmitted in any form or by any means, electronic, mechanical, photocopying, recording, or otherwise, without the express written permission of the publisher.

For permissions contact: admin@ameliadax.com

Cover by Amelia Dax

ISBN: 9781990499319

ACKNOWLEDGEMENTS

I am surrounded by the best people who encourage me
on this crazy adventure.
I am thankful to you all. All day. Every day.

And to the person who stole Judy, "Really?"

FLAT TIRE TRYST

I tried not to be bitter. Really, I did, but lately everything had a pall hanging over it thanks to my ex, Emma.

Even though I left the relationship a year ago, she still contacted me through direct messages and posts on my social media with fake accounts. Every time I blocked her, she'd pop up again using another one. It was always the same. Accusations, nothing specific but always implying people didn't know the real me. That I was deceitful, harmful, aggressive. She spread them online far and wide for everyone to hear.

The offense?

I broke up with her before she was ready to stop toying with me.

We met when I was trying to come to terms with who I was. She was my first adult girlfriend. I'd had crushes in school of course, but secondary school is not the place to come out.

She was the first person I felt I could be my true self around. I'd confided in her, and then she used my words against me.

My family and close friends knew the truth, but people I just met don't know who to believe.

I've overheard more than one conversation. "She seems nice, but where there's smoke, there is usually fire."

If I weren't so mad, I'd curl up in a ball and retreat from the world, but that was exactly what Emma wanted me to do.

She needed me to be weak so she could win this contest. This sick little game of hers that I didn't sign up for.

1

There was no fucking way I was going to let her win.

I escaped and tried to move on, but her tentacles kept reaching for me and ruining any potential relationships. I rarely got past the second date before she inserted herself as a 'concerned individual'. Which is why tonight, after work, I was heading to Fredericton to meet someone.

I wasn't sure why this crazy notion of trying to have another relationship kept entering my head. Emma was only going to try to ruin it. Even if she didn't, how was I supposed to maintain a long-distance romance when I worked two jobs?

As it was, I had to take the night off in order to meet her. I couldn't afford to miss a shift every week.

My blind date, if you want to call her that, was a friend of a friend who had been warned about my situation with Emma's lies and harassment. She still wanted to meet me. She'd been in a similar situation and thought our shared experiences could help forge a stronger foundation, even if it just turned out to be friendship. She felt we understood what the other had gone through.

I agreed.

Too nervous to hang around until it was time to leave, I decided to make the drive a mini-road trip and take the old road along the river, rather than the highway.

I loved traveling along the mostly deserted route, singing along with the radio blasting. I'd almost reached the exit to Gagetown when I heard a loud bang and the steering wheel jerked out of my hands.

I lost control of the car as it veered across the centre line. I slammed on the brakes.

The screech of the front rim on the driver's side changed as it slid from the pavement onto the gravel. My car tilted into the opposite ditch, facing oncoming traffic.

It took me a moment to remember how to breathe again and another to regain my senses enough to hit the four-way-flashers.

From the angle inside the car, I knew my driver's side front wheel was over the edge and off the road. Cursing under my breath, I slowly slid my seat backward as far as it could go and lowered the seatback to give me as much room as possible. The only way out was to crawl over the console and get out the passenger door.

It should have been fairly straightforward. Turn at the waist, use the passenger seat to pull myself up and then crawl to the other side and exit the vehicle.

However, I am not a small person. Short yes, but I've got boobs and ass for days with enough of a stomach to make me feel self-conscious… another thing to thank my ex for. Before her, I used to have a healthy sense of self-esteem.

I got myself turned over and was half sprawled over the console when the passenger door opened.

"Are you okay?" a female voice asked from just outside my vehicle.

I lowered my head and banged it against the passenger seat.

"I'm fine." My reply was muffled. I could only imagine what I looked like with my ass sticking high in the air and my back and belly fat on display because of course, the cute top I'd worn for tonight's date was riding high, exposing every part of my body I disliked.

"Oh my. Aren't you a delicious sight for sore eyes?" She whispered in awe.

"What?!" My head came up with a jerk, nearly giving myself whiplash. My jaw dropped when I saw she'd bent down. She was either unaware or uncaring that her top gaped and I was eye to eye with her perky breasts and their rosy nipples, sans bra.

"Jilly, jilly, jilly-humpers." I swore.

"What's a Jilly-humper?" Her hair shifted over her shoulders as she tilted her head. I'm sure her expression was confused.

"It's a swear word when you work with preschoolers." My laugh was awkward because of my position. Not only with my ass in the air but trying to force my gaze up to her face was physically challenging and mentally impossible. My eyes refused to move from her cleavage.

"You are absolutely perfect," she said half to herself and then stood, "I'm not sure if I can help you get to this side of the car," she said with a laugh, "but once you're out, we can get my truck and I'll haul you out of the ditch so you have all four wheels on the ground again."

"Well, three of them at least." I told her. "I'm pretty sure I shredded a tire," I responded as I pushed up from where I'd been resting on my elbows and scrambled the rest of the way across the console in the front seat. "And thank you. A tow would be wonderful."

Her hands were quick to offer support as I twisted around and could finally step out of the vehicle.

Now that I could look at her face on, I realized she was everything I wasn't. She was at least five-ten and built like a model. A willowy blonde with long luscious locks that drifted past her shoulders almost to her waist and those damn perky breasts that kept drawing my eye.

In contrast, I was barely five-foot-four and had short, dark curly hair. At least I was wearing a dressy top and a pair of longish walking shorts paired with sandals that I'd somehow managed to keep on my feet during my trek across the car.

Her look was much more farmhouse chic, a loose tank top covered by an unbuttoned plaid flannel shirt and boyfriend jeans that were streaked with dirt.

She caught my perusal and said, "Sorry I've been out working in the garden." She pointed behind her, turning slightly so I could see the shirttail of her flannel, tucked into her pocket along with a pair of leather work gloves.

At the sight of her ass, I wondered, was there anything about this woman that wasn't perky?

For a moment I didn't regret my near car accident as she held out her hand after wiping it on her shirt. "Hi. I'm Maggie. My house is just across the way." She gestured with her other hand across the street to a driveway and neatly trimmed lawn.

I couldn't believe my luck. I thought I was in the middle of nowhere. I'd probably been so distracted with keeping my car on the road that I hadn't noticed her cute little mailbox with the sunflowers painted on it.

"I'm Callie," I said as I shook her hand and then followed her to her driveway. "I'm so happy you found me. I'm pretty sure I lost my cell signal a couple of kilometers back. That'll teach me for taking the scenic route to Fredericton."

"Yeah." She grimaced. "The signal is really spotty up this way. Not enough people living here to make it worthwhile, I guess."

As we walked up the driveway, I realized why I hadn't seen her house. A hedge shielded the lawn and her lovely little log cabin from the road. It blended in so well with the landscape that it would have been impossible to see from the direction I drove. The house looked so homey with its low wrap-around-porch running along the entire front and side, shifting into a little covered walkway to get from the house to the garage.

"This is such a lovely home," I said, truly impressed. "It's exactly my idea of paradise."

She smiled. "Thank you. I love it. Moving out here seemed like a dream. I've always loved gardening." Her smile faltered for an instant. "It has its downsides. We're kind of isolated in case of an emergency." She paused and then brightened again. "For the most part, I'm content with the way things are."

She led me toward the open garage door, the interior shadowed because of the trees and the angle of the sun.

As soon as we stepped inside, I whistled at the sight of her vintage truck. "Oh, that's gorgeous."

"You like?" She grinned. "One needs to have a truck when you live out this far, and this is my baby. I've done all the maintenance on it myself."

Not that I was a huge truck person, but even I could see the old Chevy pickup, probably mid 70s was a thing of beauty. It had dark paint with a white panel along the sides. This baby was immaculate. From what I could see, there wasn't a hint of rust.

I looked between her and the truck and back. I thought about her cozy house and felt like canceling my date because I'd already found my dream woman. She might have been a year or two older than me, but she was looking at me with the same, not-so-subtle hunger that I'm sure was clear to see written in my expression.

"You look hot," she smirked at her double meaning.

At least I hoped it had a double meaning.

"Let's get something cold to drink before we pull your car out. It'll be safe. There's hardly any traffic along this road at this time of day."

6

I nodded. "That sounds wonderful." I trailed after her like a little puppy as we crossed in front of the truck, up the stairs, and through the covered walkway into her house.

Her kitchen was spacious. Brightly lit by a wide window overlooking the backyard. Tiny rainbows danced across the counter thanks to a dozen teardrop-shaped prisms that caught the sun as they hung in the window.

"I love prisms," she said when she saw me looking at them. "They always seem to hold a promise for something good to come."

"Like your own personal rainbow." I agreed as I peered between them to see her backyard was just as pretty as the front. She had a huge vegetable garden in the centre to catch all the light and shaded garden beds along each side.

The porch wrapped around the back of her house too, creating a lovely deck space. She had an old wooden swing and matching patio furniture.

"Oh, this place is to die for," I said as I gawked at her property.

"Yeah," she said with a sad smile. "Do you want something to eat?" She quickly changed the subject and opened the fridge door. There was an abundance of fresh fruit and vegetables, and a butcher-paper wrapped pack of meat. She pulled out items and put them beside what looked like homemade bread on the counter.

At the sight of the food, my stomach growled. I hadn't been able to eat lunch because I was too nervous about my date tonight.

"So that's a yes," she said with a smile and started to cut the slices of bread thick. When I started to protest about needing to watch my weight, she gave me a look that stopped me mid-sentence. "You do not have to watch your weight." She looked me up and down. "You are perfect the way you

7

are. As a matter of fact." She put the knife and the loaf of bread aside and stepped over to me, putting her hands on my shoulders. "You are the most perfectly beautiful woman I have ever seen in my life, and if you don't mind me being forward, I knew I had to have you as soon as I saw you."

"You mean with my fat ass in the air and my belly fat on display?" I tried to make it a joke.

"You say it as if it's a bad thing." She sounded confused. "I would love to have curves like yours. Instead, I'm built like a boyish twig."

I looked at her in amazement. How could someone who looked like her have such a poor opinion of herself? "Didn't you notice how I couldn't keep my eyes off your cleavage when you bent down to see if I was all right?" I asked her. "I felt like such a creep because you were trying to help me, and I was wondering how your nipples would taste in my mouth."

She stepped back as if struck, and I thought for sure I'd overstepped, and she was going to order me out of her house for being so crass.

Which, to be honest, surprised me too. I was never the instigator. After the games my ex played, I didn't even have the confidence to tell my mirror I looked nice.

Instead of kicking me out, she shrugged off her flannel shirt and pulled the hem of her T-shirt up over her head, leaving her naked from the waist up.

"I'd rather have your mouth on me than on a sandwich," she leaned forward, offering her breasts to me.

I loved the way the difference in our height worked to my advantage. I didn't have to bend far to latch on to one of her taut peaks as my hands came up around her waist and moved up to cup her breasts.

She was so responsive, her nipple grew even harder underneath my mouth as I kissed around it, paying attention to the sensitive underside of her breast, worshiping one before moving to the other.

One of her hands threaded up through my short hair, tugging at my curls, not to pull me away but to urge me closer. Directing my attention to where she needed it most.

I let her. From my point of view, there wasn't a bad spot on her body. I'd follow her lead anywhere.

"I need you," she said. "It's been so long since I've been touched like this. You're an angel sent from above. Please let me feel you."

I lifted my head to gaze into her eyes. She was calling me the angel while I had her perfect breasts in my hands.

The expression on her face validated her words. Her lips parted. Her eyes hooded as her hands stroked over my shoulders and down my sides, coming together at the front. She started undoing the buttons on my top.

I just wanted her to rip the damn thing off. I was so eager to have her hands on me. My hands came up to do exactly that when she stopped me.

"No. Let me," she smiled. "Let me take my time and explore you."

I nodded because, honestly, what could I say after a request like that?

She let her fingers duck under the seam of my low collar, their tips brushing against my skin as she unbuttoned.

My peaks were hard enough they could have sliced through the fabric on their own as she opened my shirt and pushed it from my shoulders. I let it fall to the floor, not caring if it got stomped on and wrinkled.

Underneath, I was wearing one of my best bras, just in case my blind date went well. It was padded just enough to keep my girls pushed-up high. It had a front clasp that she couldn't undo.

Her look of frustration when she couldn't figure it out right away was adorable. It was as if she'd never seen that type of clasp before.

I put my hand gently over hers and twisted it so it would unclasp.

"It's harder when you're not the one wearing it," I said with a grin.

She smiled as she lifted my breasts from their cage and nudged the fabric away. "Oh my. They are wonderful." She held them in her hands as if gauging their weight before she bent down to rain kisses over the tops. "I love how pale and pink you are." She pushed her chest towards mine and pressed our nipples together. Hers so dark and mine so pale. The perfect complement.

"Can I take you upstairs to my bedroom?" Hope glittered in her eyes.

"Absolutely." I took the hand she offered me. How was this happening to me? My mind raced with disbelief. Did I hit my head in the accident? Was I dead, and is this heaven? If so, sign me up.

She led me from the kitchen, through the living room and then up the stairs. Her bedroom encompassed the entire top floor. It was directly under the roof, as the ceiling sloped from the peak in the centre to just above the floor on either side. Her bed was centered between the windows with a gorgeous old quilt covering it.

That was all I saw before she backed me up against the wall, took my wrists and raised my arms above my head. Pinning me as she bent down to kiss me. She wasn't rough, but there was a desperation in her movements, a restrained passion. That turned me on more than I thought possible.

Our teeth clicked. Our tongues explored each other's mouths. Her knees bent, trapping me between her thighs so she could bring her chest flush against mine. The hard peaks of our breasts doing their own silent battle.

She kept one hand on my wrists, holding them in place above my head, while her other trailed past the underside of my arm and down the side of my breasts with the back of her fingers, setting my skin aflame with sensation before she flattened her palm against my side.

She slid one of her thighs between my legs, nudging my knees apart as she held me in place.

"I love the way you feel," she whispered against my lips before diving in again for another kiss.

I was so aroused I started rubbing myself against her leg like a dog in heat. I wanted to be embarrassed by my reaction, but it felt so good.

"That's it. Take your orgasm from me," she ordered as she moved her hands under my breasts and raised them up to her mouth. Her palms pressed my mounds together, pinching one nipple while she suckled the other. Goosebumps erupted where her hot mouth left wet skin when she switched sides to engulf my other breast.

My hands came down over her shoulders, and my fingers ran up through her hair, pushing her further into my chest while I humped her leg. The lacy underwear I wore added an extra layer of texture and friction that had me gasping for breath and banging my head against the wall. My vision narrowed as my body shook against her.

"Fuck me." My voice was a breathy groan as sharp waves of pleasure ignited. I rubbed against her, gripping her tightly as I chased the last vestiges of my orgasm until my legs were weak.

Her movements slowed as she held me. Bringing me gently back to earth.

It took me a minute to recover before I ordered. "Pant's off now." I pointed to the bed. "I need to taste you."

She giggled and turned toward her bed, pants off by the time she hit the mattress.

"On your back and spread your legs," I said as she coyly tried to lie on her side. My hands slid up her inner thighs, pushing her knees apart.

Her hands fluttered as if wanting to cover herself, which gave me pause. Reality crashed in. This was more than a petting session. I pulled back. "We don't have to go any farther if you don't want to."

"I want this more than anything." Her arms landed on the mattress. Her fingers splayed across the worn quilt as her knees fell open.

God, she was beautiful. Hair spread over the handmade bedspread, eager smile, and her pretty pussy drenched for me.

I put one knee on the end of the bed. "Scooch up a bit so your head is on the pillow." An instant later, I followed her up the bed and bent over to trail kisses up along the inside of her knee. Some were open mouth, others a little lick with a flick of my tongue. I loved the sounds she made.

I was more aroused than I was before my orgasm. My hand rested on her other knee. My thumb drew circles on the soft part of her flesh until I could no longer resist. I moved both hands under her thighs to hold her ass as I lowered my head to the juncture between her legs. I licked up one side of her outer lips and then did the same thing with the other.

I wrapped my arms around her slender hips to give my hands enough room to pull at her slight belly enough to force those succulent lips apart so I could have full access to her treasures.

Her entrance was so wet it glistened.

I didn't want to waste a drop. I took a long, leisurely lick from her entrance up to just before her clit.

She groaned when I stopped. Hating and loving the way I teased her. I blew on her as I drifted back toward her entrance. This time I used small leisurely licks. Up one side and then the other. Little flicks that left her gasping.

"You're torturing me," she breathed out.

I smiled against her flesh as I moved up her body, kissing every inch of her abdomen and torso as I rubbed my body against hers before placing my knee between her legs to use as a humping-post as our lips met.

In a move I wasn't expecting, she rolled me over onto my back, and she was in control again.

I didn't mind at all. I've never felt so wanted before. So necessary to someone else's pleasure.

She swivelled above me until we were head to toe. She trapped my face between her toned thighs. An instant later, she latched onto my clit and my eyes closed. The slight suction and rhythm of her tongue against that bundle of nerves sent a shock through my entire body. I cracked my head against her wrought-iron headboard.

"Sorry." Her voice was muffled between my legs. She may have been sorry I banged my head, but she wasn't sorry for the action that caused it. She went right back to what she was doing.

And I loved every minute of it.

I grabbed her ass above me and adjusted my shoulders and neck to return the favour.

Her body stiffened with shock when I surrounded her clit with my lips. I mimicked her, motion for motion, as we crept closer to release. If she did it to me, she must love it done to her. I let her lead us until the simmering tension between us exploded.

I didn't stop. I prioritized her over my orgasm until her thighs stopped shaking above me.

She collapsed on top of me before sliding to the mattress, changed her body's direction, and then crawled up to lie next to me. Her hands came up to wrap over my waist as she rested her head on my shoulder.

"I'm so glad you stopped by." Her laugh was almost a giggle.

"Best flat tire I've ever had," I agreed.

We lay together for several minutes, content just to be with each other as we watched the sunlight drift across the wall, through the prisms she had in her bedroom windows too.

"I'm going to call the woman I was meeting and cancel." I told her. Unwilling to move from this perfect spot. With the perfect person.

"No." She sat up quickly. "You can't miss your date. It's important." She began to put her clothes back on.

"It's not. Really." I sat up more slowly. "She's just a friend of a friend."

"She's going to be the best thing that ever happened to you," she said with confidence.

"Why can't you be?" I hated the whine I heard in my voice. Had I learned nothing from my ex?

Half-dressed, she walked around to my side of the bed. "I was selfish." She wrapped her arms around me. "You escaped and found hope again. I wanted to have a little part of that excitement."

"What?" I asked.

She didn't answer. "Come on. Get dressed. We have to get your car out of the ditch." She ran down the stairs. Her small breasts bounced as she disappeared from sight.

It took me longer. Rejection replaced contentment, making my movements slower. It didn't help that I couldn't find my underwear. I'd just decided to go commando when I spotted them three stairs down.

I crept down the stairs to grab them and glanced in the kitchen before turning to go back upstairs to finish dressing. I saw her standing in front of the window, playing with one of the prisms. Her shoulders shook as if she was crying.

The sight calmed me. This wasn't easy for her either.

In silence, we climbed into her vintage truck. I wasn't good at hiding my emotions, and anyone looking at me, at us, would know what we'd been doing.

It seemed like we were in her bedroom forever. The last thing I wanted to do was pull my car out of the ditch and then continue to Fredericton for a date with someone else.

Despite her refusal, I felt like I'd just found the new relationship I'd been hoping for, as if it was a blessing sent down from above.

A relationship that stemmed from a meet-cute that rivaled the most overused romantic tropes.

"How'd you meet?"

"Well, you see, she came to my rescue after my car blew a tire."

Despite my hope she'd change her mind, she backed out of her garage and headed for my car with the flat front tire hanging over the end of the steep drop-off into the ditch. Expertly, she hooked my vehicle up and then leaned over my center console to turn my car on and put it into neutral.

There was no way I could ever have reached it without climbing all the way back in. As I watched jealously as she

15

accomplished this feat, I took a moment to memorize the view of her body. The one I'd just thoroughly explored. My hands itched at my sides to feel her soft skin again.

Catching the direction of my gaze, she wagged her finger playfully at me. "That's enough of that, young lady. Let's get you moving." She cupped my face in her hands and kissed me as if she couldn't resist me either. "Stand over here where it's safe, in case the chains let go. You are too precious to risk."

I stood where she told me to in a daze.

Once she settled in her truck, she started off slow until the slack tightened and then pressed the gas pedal with enough force to make her rear tires spin slightly before gripping the road enough to ease my car backward.

Once it was clear of the ditch, I jumped in the driver's door and put it in park and shut down the engine again. I popped open the trunk with the switch on the floor, beside the one for my gas tank.

The trunk popped open, surprising her. She'd had a puzzled expression on her face when she couldn't find the lever. "I've been driving my old truck for so long, I didn't realize there was an inside switch. No wonder I couldn't open it."

Between the two of us, it took no time to change the tire. The hardest part was loosening the bolts that had been mechanically tightened after putting on my summer tires last spring.

Then it was time to go.

I tried again. "I really want to call and cancel my date tonight."

"No, go. She will be able to give you all that I can't. She will change your life in all the best ways." She hugged me tightly. "I am truly thankful you are the person I'd hoped you'd be. I'm so glad I had the chance to know you. Even if it was just for a little while."

Her kiss lingered on my lips long after I'd started my car and watched her turn into her driveway in my rear-view mirror. There were tears in my eyes at the thought of never seeing her again.

"Screw it," I said to my empty car and did a three-point turn in the middle of the road to follow her into her yard. Determined to make her see reason.

I flicked the turn signal and immediately slammed my foot on the brake. "What the actual fuck?"

Her neatly trimmed yard and long driveway had disappeared. In its place was an overgrown mess of trees and weeds. The house sat dilapidated, wraparound porch sagging and the connecting roof between the house and garage gone. The doors of the garage hung open, and her vintage truck was rusted through. It looked as if it hadn't been moved in decades.

I did the fastest one-eighty I'd ever done and sped until I reached the turnoff to Gagetown. In the gas station bathroom, I splashed cold water on my face. Not waiting for the hot water to kick in. Hell, I needed it cold anyway. "What the hell just happened?"

I glanced at my watch just to ground myself in reality. Only to see that I wasn't almost late for my date. In fact, no time had passed since my car blew its tire. If I continued on to Fredericton, I'd be over an hour early, as planned.

Had it all been a dream? Did I hit my head when I went into the ditch?

Then, her voice echoed through my mind. Statements that made no sense. "I was selfish. I just wanted to feel a bit of your hope." And, "I'm so glad you are the person I thought you'd be."

Then I knew. Without a shadow of a doubt, I knew she was the one who somehow blew my tire and stopped my car.

I dried my face and looked in the mirror only to see my lipstick, that a minute ago had been smudged off by our kisses, was again impeccable. My curls were fluffed up as if they hadn't just had a case of just-got-fucked-flatness.

Unbelieving, I raced outside to see my regular front tire was on my car. I pressed the fob button for my trunk only to see my spare tire undisturbed, still buried under my bag and the rest of the junk that permanently lived in my trunk.

I slammed the trunk closed, not sure if I had temporarily lost my mind or if I'd just had sex with some sort of ghost.

Stunned, I walked up the length of the car and sat down in the driver's seat.

That's when I saw one of the prisms from her kitchen window hanging from my rearview mirror.

KAT CAME BACK

Tony couldn't believe his luck. After years of being a bachelor and, to be honest, an awkward-as-fuck bachelor who understood computers better than people, he was thrilled when Sheila finally agreed to go out with him.

Miracle upon miracles, Tony made it past the first date and the second.

The first night she came over to his home to spend the night, he had his house spic and span. He'd done laundry and even aired out his bedroom to make sure it didn't smell like dirty socks.

After dinner, he and Sheila made out on the couch until she suggested it was time to go to the bedroom.

The bedroom.

That's when his brain woke up from its sexual anticipation haze.

Katherine, Kat for short, his lifelike sex doll was still lounging on her side of his bed. The doll had become such a fixture in his life, he hadn't thought of getting rid of her for the night.

He didn't think Sheila would find the doll's presence nearly as comforting as he did. He quickly disentangled himself from Sheila's arms.

"Just a minute, Babe." He got up, raced to the room and shoved Kat in his closet.

Luckily, earlier that afternoon, in an attempt to set a romantic mood, he'd put candles along his dresser. After shoving the doll into the closet, he took a minute to light them, thankful they gave him a reasonable excuse for leaving so abruptly.

He stumbled over his feet as he raced back to the living room and gallantly escorted his new love into the bedroom.

She sighed dreamily when she saw the lighted candles. Phew, crisis averted, he congratulated himself.

Like magnets, they moved together. Kissing and stroking each other's bodies as they stripped their clothes off.

With Kat fresh in his mind, Tony did a mental comparison between the two women as each new treasure came into focus.

Kat's tits were firmer and didn't sag, but Sheila's were warm and softer. Plus, her nipples peaked when he sucked them.

He loved how Sheila responded to him with gasps and moans of satisfaction.

Kat couldn't do that.

Sure, Sheila carried a bit more weight than the doll did, but he really didn't care because she was a real woman.

The doll never had to eat or exercise. She was the same day in and day out.

Sheila's kisses tasted of their after-dinner coffee and mint ice cream.

Even after months of use, Kat still had a lingering taste of silicone and rubberized-plastic.

Once they were naked, Sheila lay on her back on the bed. She spread her legs and put her hand over her pussy. Not out of shyness but to finger herself, inviting him to make the next move.

Not wanting to disappoint, Tony knelt on the floor ready to do something he'd never done on Kat. At first he was tentative. He'd never really gone down on a woman before. Using Sheila's moans as a guide to what felt good, he stroked his tongue along her soft flesh. Surprised at how much he enjoyed this type of foreplay.

He got right into it until she was screaming, "Right there. Don't stop."

Her legs clamped tight around his ears as her body vibrated around his head.

When she relaxed, he looked up and saw a huge grin on her face. "Keep doing it like that, and I will love you forever," she promised.

He was so proud of himself he almost forgot about his raging hard-on until it brushed against the mattress as he got to his feet.

At the sight, she spread her legs even farther. "I think we need to take care of you," she said as her eyes stayed fixed on the cock jutting out from between his legs.

Tony didn't think he'd ever been that hard as he kneeled on the bed and slid his hips between her thighs. He'd barely notched himself at her entrance before she dug her feet into the mattress and impaled herself on him.

As he buried himself inside Sheila, that's where the true difference between woman and doll became obvious.

Sheila was so hot and tight. Despite her slickness, she gripped him with inner muscles that threatened to make him come before he got fully seated within her.

He had extra-strength lube in the drawer beside his bed, but Sheila didn't need any.

Sheila shifted toward him every time he plunged inside her narrow entrance. She flexed around his cock with every stroke.

He wasn't doing all the work. It was a nice change. Still, he felt guilty. He couldn't help glancing at the closet door, knowing Kat was behind it. He knew she was just a plastic doll, but he also imagined her feeling rejected.

The thought distressed him so much Tony almost lost his boner halfway through fucking Sheila.

Sheila put her hands up to his face and brought his attention back to her. "Isn't this good for you, Babe?" She looked worried. "You're a million miles away."

His focus switched back to the woman in his bed. "I'm lost in the sensation." He leaned down to kiss her. "You feel so good." How had he managed to sound so smooth when he'd been caught thinking about another woman?

He made up for it. He pressed in for an extra beat every time their hips met, giving her the ability to rub her clit against him, which she seemed to love.

Lifting her ankles to his shoulders, he leaned close over her to drive himself deeper into her wetness.

He loved watching her eyes roll back as he tucked her foot under his chin and used his thumb to rub her clit. Her reaction was immediate.

She let go, arching her back with fingers gripping the bedspread as if it was her last tether to reality. She milked his cock until he felt his own orgasm explode inside her.

Later, as they snuggled in bed, she fell asleep first. He couldn't help but glance over toward the closet door and noticed it had somehow popped open a crack. Too drowsy to think much of it, he drifted off to sleep.

The next morning, he had another near miss with the doll because Sheila was about to open his closet door to get one of his button-up shirts to wear while they had breakfast. As much as he wanted to see her in one of his white dress shirts with her dark nipples poking at the light-coloured fabric, he grabbed one of his hoodies from the drawer instead.

She looked so adorable bundled up in his clothing. She loved it too and nearly skipped out to the kitchen to make the coffee.

Tony felt torn. Guilty for being resentful in the moment of Kat's presence in his closet, getting in the way of a perfect morning fantasy of his sexy girlfriend cooking for him in a nearly see-through white shirt.

After Sheila left his house, Tony decided it was time to get rid of the doll. He just had to figure out how. She wasn't a blow-up doll. She was built like a mannequin, full size and solid all the way through. He couldn't just deflate her and store her in the garage.

As he contemplated what to do with her, his memory started replaying all the good times they'd shared. Even though he just had sex with Sheila again this morning, he already had another erection.

What harm could there be if he had Kat one last time?

He retrieved Kat from the closet and laid her down on the bed. Her wide-eyed gaze made him feel even more guilty about what he knew he was about to do. But he had to dispose of the doll if he wanted to keep Sheila.

Sheila was his future, and Kat had to be his past. He was still arguing with himself, trying to find another way out of his situation when he realized he was already lubed up and balls deep in the doll.

Damn, he really had to pay more attention to the women in his life.

He clicked the buttons on the back of her neck to start the motor for the rolling motion within her channel to simulate the feel of a live woman.

Kat was so special, he thought as he slid into her comforting depths. He raised her legs up and pumped slowly into her special rubberized channel designed to feel like actual skin. It gripped him just the same as it always had, and while her hips didn't move like Sheila's, he enjoyed the steady friction.

In and out, he bent forward and fondled her tits. Sucking her nipples, and again found himself comparing the doll to Sheila, and honestly, they were coming out as a tie.

Both had their advantages.

Both had their disadvantages.

He looked deep into Kat's eyes as he plowed into her. Yet, Sheila lingered in the back of his mind, increasing his arousal as if he were having them both at once

There was no recrimination in Kat's gaze. The smile on her face never wavered as he plunged into her again and again until he felt his balls tighten.

He let loose with a deep growl. His hands gripped Kat's hips as he pumped into her. Releasing his load.

He pulled out of Kat's depths with the same guilty feeling as last night when he and Sheila finished having sex.

At this point he wasn't sure who was the main squeeze and who was the side chick. He pondered his dilemma as he cleaned out the doll and wondered if there was a way to keep them both.

Despite his earlier decision, he wasn't quite ready to part with Kat yet, so he tucked her out of sight and draped a moving blanket over her in the garage every time Sheila came over.

It was only a temporary solution. Sheila was soon there every weekend, and then they were talking about moving in together. He was going to have to do something. He didn't want her to find a naked Kat in his home, even if she was just a doll.

Finally, they had a date. Sheila would move in at the end of the month.

Tony procrastinated as long as he could. He'd have sex with Sheila when she spent the night and fuck Kat when she didn't. Then it was moving day, and he'd run out of time.

Sheila had dropped off a load of personal items she didn't want the movers to handle, and he was going to follow her back to her place to offer moral support while the hired hands packed up the rest of her life.

After she left, he realized too late that Kat wasn't going to fit easily in his trunk.

While her legs were movable, they didn't bend quite far enough. When he'd bought her, she was in a box that was easy to shove through the folded-down back seat. It seemed wrong to do it when she was naked and vulnerable.

He wasn't a monster.

Plus, if someone looked into his car and saw her laying half in the trunk, they'd call the cops.

He went back into his house and grabbed another sweatshirt from his drawer. He partially dressed her, put the hood up and then put her in his passenger seat and hoped no one looked too closely as he drove her outside the city limits to bury her in a picturesque spot he knew of.

Sure, he could have shoved her in the local dump, but he felt she deserved a proper burial. After all, she'd been his girlfriend for over a year.

Knowing the place he'd picked out should be deserted at that time of day, he put a shovel and tarp in his trunk. The tarp was to wrap her up, so she wasn't left exposed to the elements.

As he drove along the road, guilt ate away at him. He knew he was being silly because she was just a doll, but they'd had some fun over their time together, and he felt bad about abandoning her.

He loved Sheila and couldn't wait to build a life with her, and he knew Sheila would never tolerate sharing his passion with a plastic doll.

The choice had to be made.

He still remembered the day he stumbled into her, quite literally. He was at the sex shop looking for a new flesh-light when he saw his ex-girlfriend. He shrank back behind a display and tripped. Kat, the life-sized sex-doll, caught him in her open arms. Giving him a chance to regain his footing.

Her combination of perceived stability and solid strength appealed to him. He knew he had to have her.

He waited until his ex and her new boyfriend left the store and then he slid his credit card across the counter to make Kat his very own.

Ahead on the highway, the few cars ahead of him slowed.

Tony swore. There was a roadblock up ahead. Cops were on both sides of the road checking vehicles. He couldn't be caught with Kat in the passenger seat. He worked with these guys often, and he'd never hear the end of it. So, he did what any emotionally mature adult would do. He undid Kat's seatbelt and reached in front of her to open the car door as soon as he put the car in park.

With one big push, she went flying. He'd driven close enough to the guardrail that she hit it and flipped right over.

He pulled back out onto the road, thankful no one seemed to notice what he'd just done.

Apparently, the cops were looking for a child who'd been taken by a non-custodial parent. He wished the guys, "Good luck" on their search and then drove quickly to Sheila's apartment.

He meant to go back and get Kat and give her a proper burial, but he got busy with Sheila as she unpacked and reorganized their now shared living space. A few days passed, and he'd forgotten all about her.

One morning nearly two weeks later, Sheila asked him to go get steaks out of the freezer in the garage. They could thaw while they were at work, and she'd cook them for supper that night.

He opened the connecting door between the house and garage and nearly shit his pants.

There was Kat. She stood against Sheila's car, leaning away from him over the hood, with her ass sticking out and her wide eyes looking at him over her shoulder in invitation.

She was still wearing his sweatshirt, although it was a little muddier than it had been, and the once smooth flesh on the back of her legs was a little scuffed up from her fall over the guardrail. She had twigs tangled in her long hair.

He stifled a scream and a boner at her appearance and quickly closed the door behind him. He raced to grab Kat off the car and shoved her into the back seat of his vehicle.

"What the actual fuck." He muttered to himself. Had the guys seen him ditch the doll and decide to play a prank? Didn't matter, he had to get rid of the doll before Sheila saw it.

"Did you find the steaks?" Sheila called from the house.

"Yep, I've got them. I just had to do something else too," he said as he grabbed the meat from the freezer.

He gave his car one last look to make sure Kat was out of sight before he closed the garage door. Thankful that he was going to be the first one to leave for work today, just in case Kat inexplicably popped up again.

Before he climbed into his car, he threw a blanket over the doll and put his shovel back in the trunk along with the tarp he'd originally intended to wrap her in before the cop's roadblock derailed his plans the other day.

Even though her reappearance freaked him out, he still didn't want her lying exposed in the ground. This time he was determined to bury her properly.

27

As soon as his car cleared his driveway, he called his office and told them he'd be late. He lied and said he needed to fix a flat and then headed out to his original destination for Kat's burial. A nice shady spot with a view of the lake. A perfect resting place for his pseudo girlfriend.

"I'm sorry, Kat," he said as he drove. "I really hate doing this, but Sheila can't know about you. I have a chance to have a life partner. If you were real, it would be a different story, but we both know that you're made of plastic and silicone and were manufactured in a factory somewhere."

This time he made it to the spot without any problems. It took a bit more effort to dig the hole than he expected. The smooth soles of his dress shoes didn't help as they slid off the tip of the shovel as he dug. They were an absolute mess by the time he was finished, but at least that would validate his story about getting a flat tire in the mud.

He turned to get Kat from the back seat. Her knees were bent and her ass was sticking up in the perfect angle for him to enter her.

And he was only a man.

Her perfect ass, one that he had fucked so many times in the past. It was like she was purposefully offering him forgiveness in the form of one more for the road.

His cock jumped at the invitation, not caring that he didn't have any lube. He could feel pre cum dripping from the tip of his prick. It was going to stain the front of his pants if he didn't do something fast.

Wanting to avoid the extra time needed to go home and change, he pulled out his cock and started jacking it. Spreading the moisture over his broad head before he leaned into the car and pulled her hips close against him and entered her from behind.

It was dry at first, but her smooth walls welcomed him anyway as he plunged into her, pulled out and plunged in deeper. It took a few strokes, but once she warmed up, he felt her perfect tension around his cock as he realized just how much he'd missed her. He pounded into her depths, careful not to bump her head on the opposite car door.

After the stress of Kat's reappearance that morning followed by the unexpected pleasure of this middle of the woods quickie, he knew he wasn't going to last long. Vainly, he tried to hold his dress pants up so they wouldn't fall in the muddy ground at his feet.

He felt the tingle spread along the back of his legs and up his spine. Pants forgotten, he gripped her hips with both hands and pulled her against him in a rhythm that got faster and harder as he got close to exploding. Wave after wave of release shot out into Kat's ass until it was frothing around the base of his cock.

When he caught his breath, he leaned over her back and hugged her. If he was honest, in that moment he loved her as much as he did Sheila. Just in a different way.

Finally, he returned to the task at hand. He straightened her limbs and put the hoodie back on her properly. He couldn't bring himself to take the hoodie from Kat. It was hers now. He wrapped her in the tarp and placed her perfect body in the hole he'd prepared.

He even said a prayer. She may not have been human, but she was as real as any other girlfriend he'd ever had.

He buried her, then saw some late flowers blooming nearby and picked them to put on top of her as if it was truly a grave. Then he got back into his car and drove to work.

The next morning, he asked Sheila if she wanted him to grab something from the freezer. He laughed at his paranoia, but after the day before he wasn't going to take any chances.

She thought for a moment and said, "I think maybe the package of ground beef. We'll do spaghetti tonight."

As he went out to the garage, he saw Sheila smile as if congratulating herself on winning the boyfriend lottery by finding someone who was willing to share the mental load and actively participate in anticipating household requirements. This made him feel good, if not a little guilty for having ulterior motives for being so thoughtful.

Almost afraid to look, he relaxed when he stepped into the garage, and it was empty of unwanted visitors.

Sheila's car was pristine, and his still had a little mud on the tires from yesterday, but there was no sign of his sex doll anywhere.

Relieved, he grabbed the hamburger from the freezer and headed back into the house.

As usual, he was the first to leave for work. He climbed into his car, pressed the button on his visor to open the garage door, and when he looked in the rearview mirror to back out, he slammed on his brakes in shock.

Kat sat in the back seat. She was still wearing his hoodie although it was a bit dirtier now, hiked up over her hips. Her legs spread wide, one hand positioned over her pussy as if she had been fingering herself, and the other hand at her mouth with her index finger tugging slightly at the edge of her lip.

The tarp was neatly folded on the seat beside her.

He didn't know what to do. His brain stopped working, and he was freaking the fuck out.

This had gone beyond a prank. No one knew where he'd buried her unless they had put a GPS on his car. They wouldn't know that he'd buried her or disposed of her at all. He'd told no one about his dilemma with the sex-doll.

He needed another plan. He looked frantically around as his car idled half in and half out of the garage. He didn't have a lot of time. That's when he saw his weights from when he'd dismantled his workout room in the garage to make space for Sheila's car.

There was a lake near where he'd buried Kat yesterday. This could work.

He exited the car and grabbed a couple of twenty-five-pound dumbbells and two forty-five pound disks. The doll only weighed eighty pounds, so one-hundred-and-forty pounds of weight should keep her submerged until the lake froze.

He grabbed a rope and his work boots, hopped back into his vehicle and drove quickly to the same area of woods where a long wooden pier jutted out into the lake until it was deep enough for the kids to dive from in the summer.

The weatherman was calling for snow tomorrow, so it wouldn't take long for the lake to ice over once the temperature started staying below freezing.

He sent an apology text to his boss for coming in late a second day in a row and hoped he'd come up with a reasonable excuse by the time he got there.

When he got to the lake and walked around the car to pull her from the back seat, she had toppled over. The bottom hem of the hoodie was up over her tits and her legs still spread wide. One leg hanging in the footwell and the other braced over the back of the seat with her ankle hooked over the headrest.

Before he could talk himself out of it, his dress pants were down around his knees, and his cock was notched at her entrance.

This time she was face up, so he nuzzled into her neck and enjoyed the feel of her firm mounds under his fingers squeezing them gently and pinching her nipples that were shaped so differently from Sheila's.

Both were perfect in their own way.

He pulled her torso toward him to let her tits drag across his chest with the force of each thrust. Loving the feel of her against him as he drove into her for the last time.

Dear God, let it be the last time. His heart faltered at the thought of discovering her again tomorrow. Until he reassured himself, she wouldn't be able to escape from under the pier. Even if someone followed him by GPS. This time they'd have no idea where he'd put her. There would be no freshly dug hole to give her location away.

Satisfied with his plan, he refocused on the way Kat's body engulfed him. He loved the way the angle of her legs tightened her channel around his cock. Every 'last time' he fucked her felt better than the one before. It was getting harder and harder to let her go, even though he knew he couldn't keep her. Sheila would never understand, let alone approve.

He gazed into Kat's eyes, his ever-loyal sex doll, as he thrust into her again and again. Revelling in the friction of her lifelike skin, making her feel so warm as she gripped him. His strokes grew shorter and more frantic as he desperately tried to hold off and not cum too soon.

But it felt so good.

His movements became more erratic until he blew his load.

And then it was done.

He wanted to lay content in her arms, give himself a chance to recover and then do it all over again before sinking her into the water. The thought and the chill air made him shiver.

Reluctantly, he pushed away and pulled his pants up. He changed his shoes into work boots and, while she was still in the car's warmth, wrapped the tarp around her again after straightening her limbs.

He adjusted the hoodie over her hips again. It took him two trips to carry the weights to the end of the wooden wharf, and then he carried her like a bride about to cross the threshold. The irony wasn't lost on him.

He wound the ropes around her entire body, making sure that the weights were securely attached. The twenty-five pound dumbbells on each end and the two forty-five-pound disks attached in the middle. Her hourglass shape would help keep them in place. The last thing he did was tie both ends of the tarp closed to ensure she couldn't slide out in case the other ropes loosened.

He apologized profusely as he dropped her into the water, pushing her descent on an angle to keep her hidden under the wooden wharf.

Whoever found her next spring would have quite the story to tell, but he'd never hear it. There was no way to tie the doll's presence to him.

He finally made it to work, even more distracted today than he had been the day before.

He didn't sleep well, plagued with nightmares about the doll reappearing. Despite his intention to be up early, Sheila was the first one out of bed.

He woke in a panic and then relaxed when he heard Sheila in the kitchen. Curiosity made him get up to see who she was talking to this early.

He took a quick shower, still wanting to check the garage, just in case. Then he got dressed and headed down to the kitchen.

He froze in the doorway. There, sitting at the kitchen table still in his hoodie with her hair soaking wet, was Kat.

Sheila hovered over her, drying her hair with a towel, urging her to warm up with the cup of coffee in front of her as if she could actually drink it.

Sheila saw him standing there. "Look who I found outside. The poor dear was soaking wet in the rain. She was going to catch the death of a cold," Sheila said to me as she continued to dry Kat's hair.

And he'd swear to God, the doll smirked.

DEAD MEN CAN FUCK

Today was the day, Kara thought as she climbed out of bed. She'd arrived at the bed-and-breakfast last night after an hour-long drive up from the city. Now, she had all day and part of tomorrow to figure out if she was communicating with a ghost, or if she was losing her mind.

A short while later, she pulled a roast beef sandwich from her small cooler along with an apple and put it into one of the large pockets of her windbreaker and a small bottle of orange juice in the other.

She said goodbye to the hostess and started her trek up the hill to Harvey's old farm.

Harvey, she thought to herself with a smile.

She felt so close to him even though she wasn't certain if he was a ghost or hallucination. She'd communicated with him last month when she'd stayed at this same bed-and-breakfast on a weekend getaway.

Once she was home again, she'd done some research and concluded that her recent companion was Harvey Rushman. A local farmer, who died almost two centuries ago when his house burned down. The bed-and-breakfast had been part of his brother's property at the base of the hill. Her quest was to see if she could find any more clues to confirm her theory and, more importantly, confirm his current existence as a ghost.

She was spurred on by the incredible dream she had of him last night.

She'd been running across a field toward an old-fashioned log cabin with a man standing at the front door. She recognized it could be her anticipation getting the better of her, but as a result of that dream, she was convinced

Harvey would be waiting for her at the top of the hill where his farmhouse once stood.

Alder bushes grew over most of the track leading to the old homestead. In many places, there wasn't a path at all. Twice she had to detour through the woods for a few metres to avoid large anthills blocking the way.

Harvey trailed behind her as she walked up the hill toward his old homestead. He wished he could tell her that yes, she was right. He was a ghost. More importantly, her interest, while flattering, wasn't going to get them anywhere.

He already regretted the impulse that had made him bend close to see what she'd been reading last month. The cover suggested a romance, but the section he'd seen as he walked behind her, had his cock hard and his breathing laboured within a few sentences.

Somehow, she'd felt his breath on her neck. No one had ever noticed his existence before.

By the time her weekend was done, they'd found a way to communicate with each other. Simple messages written in condensation on the cold window.

Back to his current dilemma as he followed behind her. Yes. He wanted answers. Why was he forced to stay in this hellish half-life existence? How much longer did he have to endure this torture of watching everyone else live their lives? Still, he wasn't convinced this trip up memory lane was the way to find those answers.

He had been back to his farm once in the century since he died, on the one-year anniversary of the fire that destroyed his home and caused his death. Unnoticed, he'd joined his mother and brother as they did a pilgrimage to his farm.

He had been looking for answers then too. Staring at the charred remnants of his home from across the meadow had been all he could take. He couldn't force himself to go any closer.

Standing there, seeing the ruins that had once been his life, made it impossible to escape the reality of what had happened. That day, after months of hope, he finally understood. This wasn't just some horrible nightmare.

Now, almost two hundred years later, he was making the same journey again, while ridiculing himself for the insane hope that this time, with Kara beside him, maybe things would be different.

Oblivious to his lagging, Kara continued ahead, her cheeks flushed from the cool October air and the anticipation of what lay ahead. Replaying her dream in her mind, she could not stop smiling. She knew, just knew, something amazing was going to happen.

Realizing that he was falling behind, Harvey jogged until he caught up with her.

"I still think this is a bad idea," he said to himself as they rounded the final bend in the road, leaving the trees behind.

"Harvey, stop worrying so…" Kara stopped abruptly and looked in the direction of his voice. "Harvey?" her voice squeaked.

"Kara?" The sound of his own voice had shocked him too. "Oomph." He made a frantic grab for the woman who had just flung herself in the direction of his voice and almost missed him completely.

Laughing, he hugged her against him for a long moment before setting her back on the ground, keeping her wrapped securely in his arms.

"Next time you try that you had better make sure you know exactly where I'm standing. Or if I'm standing there at all or you'll end up on that cute little rear end of yours."

He chuckled. "Just because you can suddenly hear me doesn't mean I have a body."

Kara scoffed. She wasn't concerned in the slightest. "Harvey, I can't believe it. I can hear you and look." She reached up with her hands to cup his face. "I can touch you."

Recalling the near intimacy they'd shared in her dream, she raised her face, stood on her tiptoes and planted a huge kiss on the corner of his mouth. Quickly, she readjusted her aim and tried again. This time, she hit her target.

Harvey's shock made his body tense before his arms tightened around her, and he kissed her back.

Just as he was getting into the swing of the incredible turn of events, the feel of her lips against his and the way their bodies fit perfectly together, she abruptly let him go.

She fumbled for a second as she reached for his hand, then once she had him firmly in her grasp, tugged him along, forcing him to run beside her across the overgrown meadow to where his house had once stood.

This time Harvey's enthusiasm and pace matched hers as they made their way to the crumbled remains of his home's foundation. He was relieved to see time had softened the horrific remains of the fire. The only evidence left was a raised rectangle of large, moss-covered stones. To Harvey's surprise, his barn was still standing. Its roof was gone, but the four walls remained upright, albeit listing together in unison at an awkward angle.

The dread he'd been feeling flowed out of him. With so few reminders left, he knew he could handle being here again.

He took her hand. "Come on, Kara, I'll give you the grand tour."

They walked closer to where his cabin once stood. A tree had grown inside the foundation. He chuckled to himself as past and present overlapped in his mind. It created an image of the full-grown tree growing in the middle of where his kitchen had once been. He pictured it jutting out through the roof of his home.

"What's so funny?"

Startled, Harvey looked at her. "I keep forgetting you can hear me. It's been a long time since anyone has." He pulled her into his arms and dropped a chaste kiss on the top of her head before he paused to nod at the tree as if she could see him too. "I was laughing because that tree is growing in the middle of what used to be my kitchen."

Almost exactly where I collapsed the night I died, he added to himself, making sure he did not speak those words aloud for Kara to hear. "I was just picturing what it would look like if my house was still there."

Kara looked thoughtfully at the tall fir tree. "At least you wouldn't have to go searching for a Christmas tree every year." She deadpanned.

She felt his laughter rumble in his chest just before the sound escaped from his throat. She liked the way he laughed. It was genuine. For that matter, she liked his voice. It was deep with just a touch of roughness. Harvey had the kind of voice she could listen to all night long and never grow tired of the sound. It was too bad she couldn't see him. She'd hoped he'd appear when they got to his old home.

She could hear and touch him. That would have to be enough.

As they walked, the sun rose higher in the sky, enveloping them in its warmth. It was a beautiful autumn day. Standing where Harvey's front porch used to be, Harvey reminisced about how he used to be able to see the river past his horse paddock.

He was beginning to feel like his old self. He felt strong and in control.

Kara found a warm spot sheltered from the cool breeze and sat down. Harvey sat beside her as she took off her windbreaker and lay back on it. He laid down too, propping himself up on his arm.

"Am I ever out of shape," Kara stated ruefully as she looked down at her tired limbs. "After all of that walking, I'm about ready to take a nap." She closed her eyes as if to prove her point.

Harvey slowly examined her from head to toe. He lightly trailed his fingers along her jaw and down her neck until the collar of her turtleneck got in the way, preventing him from continuing.

"I don't know, but you look like you're in pretty good shape to me," he said as he moved his hand to begin lazily tracing circles on her stomach. He smiled when he heard her sharp inhale.

Had she protested, even a bit, he would have stopped immediately. Logically, he knew this was happening too fast, but instead of slowing him down, Kara did the opposite.

She reached for him.

Since she still couldn't see him, Kara found it better to keep her eyes closed. Less conflicting information went to her brain as her fingers moved over the flannel-covered muscle of his shoulder then behind his head to play with the silken threads that curled over his collar. She threaded her fingers through his wavy hair and closed her hand around the back of his neck to pull him toward her as she raised her lips to meet his.

Tentatively at first, their lips tasted each other.

Harvey's conscience tried one last time to make him back off. This was not how his mother raised him.

His heart said otherwise. This is Kara, how can it be wrong? He slid his hand up to cup her breast and knead the firm flesh beneath her light sweater.

It responded with a tantalizing glimpse of its hardened peak through the clingy fabric. Breaking away from her lips, Harvey shifted so that he could suckle her through her sweater.

Kara was surprised at the rush of need he aroused in her. She pushed him away, long enough for her to pull her turtleneck over her head, exposing the paper-thin wisp of lace that barely concealed her flesh.

Never before had she been so bold, almost aggressive, in her advances. She felt Harvey shift his weight as he leaned over her and began kissing a trail that started at her lips, moved along her jaw to the sensitive spot just behind her ear.

The combination of his strong lips and soft beard made her groan aloud. She gripped his shoulders and arched her back to get close enough to rub her aroused body against his. Harvey was magic. Never before had she felt so uninhibited, so free.

Harvey lifted his head to see her hair had come loose from her ponytail, wildly framing her face. Her lips were already swollen from his kisses. He took a deep breath.

"My God, woman, what have you done to me? We have to stop now, or I won't be able to."

Kara said nothing. Instead, she reached up to undo the buttons on his shirt. When she finished, she pushed the fabric out of the way to give her hands unlimited access to explore his hard, hair-roughened chest and abs. She could feel the erratic pounding of his heart as he tried to keep himself under control.

He relaxed against the ground to let her take the lead. He had never been this aroused before in his life, and then she adjusted her body until she was straddling his lower half and was practically purring as she rubbed her naked breasts against his chest.

Harvey looked up to see that she had undone the front clasp of her bra. Her perfect breasts seemed to beg for his touch. He was just about to oblige when Kara raised her torso to give herself room to slide her palms over his abs to reach the fastening of his pants.

Quickly undoing the top one, she slid her hand inside and heard Harvey grit his teeth, "Kara honey, it'll be all over in two seconds if you don't stop what you're doing."

Obediently, she removed her hand and let her fingers trail back up his torso. "I guess it's been a while, huh?"

"About two hundred years, give or take a decade," he said as he pulled her hand away from his body so he could catch his breath. "I had no idea it could be like this."

"It's the same for me. No one has ever made me feel the way you do." She caught her bottom lip between her teeth when she felt his hand slide down past the waistband of her jeans. What she had been about to say completely vanished from her mind along with any other coherent thought as Harvey moved their bodies so he could stretch out beside her.

He wound his arms around her, holding her close. He could feel her breasts crushed against his chest as they kissed leisurely, easing back from the feeling of urgency.

At least, until she shifted boldly entwining her legs with his.

Before he knew it, he was on his back again. Looking up, he thought he would drown in the depths of passion he saw reflected in her eyes.

Using her legs to pin his lower half, Kara worked her way down his body, tasting along his collarbone. Teasing her cheek with the hair on his chest. A playful nip here and a tug there until her fingers were again at the fastening of his pants.

This time she wasted no time undoing them. She pulled herself up slightly, allowing him only enough room to raise his hips to slide the fabric of his trousers down his legs. Silently, she thanked whatever entity ensured he wasn't wearing one of those old-fashioned one-piece pair of long-johns.

Harvey gasped as the cool air hit his overheated body.

Once he was completely naked, Kara moved until she knelt between his legs. She took her time working her way back up his body. She loved knowing she was affecting him as much as he affected her.

The muscles in his legs tensed as he dug his heels into the ground in reaction to her nibbling a path up the inside of his thigh. She let her bare breasts caress his calves. The light hair on his legs teased her skin, making each point of contact electric, sending her own nerve endings into overdrive.

As her mouth came closer to his crotch, he began to squirm, "Karaaa." He moaned through clenched teeth as he reached down to pull her up before he embarrassed himself.

In one swift movement, he twisted them around, so she was under him.

"Turn-about is fair-play, my love," he said as he began his own exploration. He held her prisoner as he stripped away the last of her clothing.

Straightening, he gazed down at her. "You are the most beautiful woman I have ever seen." Gently, he lowered himself, bracing his weight on one elbow while he stroked her with his other hand until her skin broke out in goosebumps.

His hands caressed their way up her legs, before lightly circling the juncture between her thighs then pressed inside with short strokes until she was soaked with arousal. With the tips of his fingers roughened by years working the land, he teased her until she was lifting off the ground, trying to increase the pressure of his touch to get relief.

"Now, Harvey," she ordered. "I can't take this anymore. I need you now." Desperately, she grabbed his muscled ass and pulled him to her.

"Your wish is my command, love," he whispered as he entered her tight channel, feeling himself surrounded by her flexing muscles that threatened to make him cum before he was fully inside.

Kara's legs wrapped themselves tightly around him, pulling him in deeper.

For a moment, he pushed back against them. He had to stop moving or he would finish right there. He breathed deeply to regain control, so he wouldn't ruin it for her.

Thankfully, Kara understood and stopped moving. She remained still until he slowly started to pull out and slide back in. With each entry, he sank further into her, marvelling at the way she moved with him.

As if she could not get enough of him.

Kara met each thrust with one of her own. Tiny explosions burst through her as their bodies moved together, each one more powerful than the one before.

Completely out of control and oblivious to the world around them, the rhythm of their slick bodies got faster and harder until Harvey let out a guttural moan.

His body stiffened, and his cock pulsed inside her.

Kara's voice mixed with his as she tightened in spasms around him. She held on, not wanting to let him go as he slid to the side before collapsing on the field beside her.

Wrapped tightly in each other's arms, they drifted off to sleep. Kara was the first to rouse. She felt the warmth of the sun on her bare skin. Muscles she hadn't used in a while ached pleasantly, while others were already perking up as she felt Harvey's body still curled around her.

His arm draped possessively over her, and his cock, even in slumber, bobbed gently against her leg as if making it clear he was ready for another go.

With a joke on her lips about his gentle snoring, Kara was momentarily nonplussed when she opened her eyes to look at her lover and not see him.

Even after everything they'd just done, he still wasn't visible.

She must have jolted in surprise because he was suddenly awake.

He pulled her closer to him, but neither seemed to be in a hurry to speak. Together they lay, each lost in their own thoughts. The tall grass sheltered them from the fall breeze, and they both fell back asleep.

This time, Harvey was the first to wake. He let his hand wander, caressing the soft skin of her arm as it lay possessively across his chest. Without speaking, he shifted, allowing his fingers to again find her breast.

Kara moaned softly as he teased her. Reciprocating, she moved her hand in slow, tantalizing circles along his chest. Gradually her fingers drew lower and lower until she discovered he was ready and waiting. She quirked her eyebrow in his direction as she weighed his heaviness in the palm of her hand.

"Kara honey, what do you expect? It's been almost two centuries since I've had sex." Harvey lowered his head, taking her lips by surprise and offering no option for escape.

Hmmm, I've finally found an advantage to being this way, he thought to himself.

A low, sexy rumble of male laughter sounded in her ear as Harvey nibbled his way down the side of her throat. He didn't want to miss an inch of her body. Knowing she liked the feel of his hair, he let his chest press against her as he crept lower, to take one breast in his mouth. Then, he kissed his way over to the other and then down over her stomach until he nudged her knees wider apart in order to fit his shoulders between them. He loved that she was already wet for him, acknowledging his cum from last time was partially to blame. It didn't stop him from flattening his tongue against her entrance and giving her a long lick before flicking his tongue in shorter strokes until her hips were chasing after his mouth to get the pressure she needed. He stilled and let her use his mouth as she needed, placing his palms under her ass for support.

Her movements grew erratic, and her moans echoed across the field. When she let go, he smiled as if he had just won a prize.

Then he rose up over her and stroked himself.

"Where did you go?" she asked, confused.

He realized it was the first time since she had jumped into his arms when they arrived at his farm that their bodies weren't touching in some way. With a grin, he pressed the tip of his cock to her entrance and slid inside.

"Oh, that's where you are." Her grin matched his.

Like before, she planted her feet and met each of his strokes with one of her own. Giving a little swivel against his pelvic bone each time he entered her.

He began to pause every time he drove into her, allowing her more time to take her pleasure from him. He was rewarded with her clenching around him like a vice until

46

he couldn't take it any longer and exploded. This time he barely had the strength to shift to the side before collapsing.

Afterward, they lay napping again like two wood nymphs in the noon sun until the wind shifted, exposing their naked skin to the cool October wind.

After they got dressed and were just about ready to head back down to the bed-and-breakfast, Kara began to laugh. Harvey looked askance as she plopped herself back down half beside him, half on where he sat on the beaten down grass since she still couldn't see him.

"What's so funny?" he asked.

Kara was laughing too hard to tell him. She simply held up her badly wrinkled windbreaker. Finally, wiping the tears of mirth from her eyes, she reached into her pocket and pulled out a squished lump of what had once been her sandwich. The homemade bread and sandwich filling had been no match for their energetic play. It had been squished beyond recognition with mustard oozing out from where the zip-closure burst under the weight of their bodies.

Like misbehaving teens, they tried to remove all the dried leaves and grass from her hair. After all, she still had to face the hostess at the bed-and-breakfast when she went back down the hill.

RECLAIMING HIS WIFE

It had been a tough year. Charles, my husband of thirty years, died suddenly last fall, and I've been lonely ever since.

It wasn't the loss of companionship that brought me down. Our friends rallied around me to make sure I wasn't left alone too much.

The biggest problem I faced was that he was so young when he died, only fifty-three. He had a huge appetite for bedroom fun, and I've really missed it since his death.

I've expanded my collection of battery-operated toys and watched more porn than I had in my entire life before his demise, but I really miss the physical touch of another person.

Toys are great, but they're not human. They can't anticipate your needs.

There's just something about having that warm body brush up against your back, or front, depending on the position. The strength of their hands around your ankles or stolen moments in the shower, or on the kitchen counter when you're trying to cook supper.

Toys just can't replace a man's touch, at least in my humble opinion.

It took a while to get over the whole mental hump of finding someone else to be intimate with. At first, even the thought of having sex with someone who wasn't Charles left me feeling guilty, as if I was cheating.

I eventually had to resign myself to the fact that Charles wasn't here anymore, and he wasn't coming back. The last thing he'd want is for me to be lonely or hurting. So, I bit the bullet and decided to try online dating.

Before you roll your eyes at me, you've got to understand. Everyone still expected me to be devastated over my husband's death. Yes, of course I was, but it's been almost a year.

While I've started to get the comments of, "Oh you'll find somebody else, you're still young." if I dared to mention I found a man attractive, the shocked and horrified expressions on people's faces told me no one else was ready for me to move on yet.

And to be truthful, I didn't really want a relationship. I just needed sex. Oh my God, did I ever need sex.

I created a profile on one of those websites aimed at finding hook-ups instead of new relationships. Which wasn't ideal. I think my ultimate goal would be to have someone who I could hang out with, give each other a great orgasm or two and then go back to my own home… alone.

At the end of the day, I wasn't ready to be with somebody in a full relationship, yet one-night stands had never been my thing.

Sure, I had a couple of them before I met my Charles, but they hadn't been voluntary. Guys always seemed to make promises to get into your pants and then disappear like a puff of smoke before you finished dressing.

One Friday night, I was a little desperate. The toys weren't cutting it anymore. I started browsing the hook-up site just to see what was out there.

It didn't take long for me to get my first message. It was a dick pic. There was no "Hello." or "How you doing?" just a picture of his penis.

It reminded me of a Canadian comedian, Erica Sigurdson, who I'd heard years ago when she said she didn't understand why men sent pictures of their cocks because really it was like looking at instructions for an un-assembled piece of IKEA furniture. It was proof he had the necessary equipment, but that was it.

Assuming of course, it was really a picture of him and not a random dick off the internet.

I ignored the photo and kept scrolling.

It was easy to see I wasn't the only one looking for love on a Friday night.

A few of the guys I swiped on to express my interest, swiped on me too. Then nothing. They just sat there, as if expecting me to make the first move or, most likely, spent the evening swiping every woman they found even slightly attractive, vainly hoping one would message them.

Moving on.

It was fifteen minutes and twice as many notifications before I got my first proper message…with words. It was amazing how quickly my bar lowered. I was actually a little excited that he spoke in full sentences and asked something besides, "What's your favourite position?"

We chatted back and forth for a few minutes before he suggested we meet up.

Considering the site I was on, I knew we weren't meeting for coffee, and I didn't really want him to come to my house, so I answered. "Sure, where do you want to meet?"

He mentioned a hotel just outside the city centre, not far from the highway.

The hotel itself was one I was familiar with, and it had a good reputation for clean rooms and a decent bar-style restaurant on the ground level. It wasn't one of the sleazy, pay by the hour places further out on the highway.

Knowing I could be on the hook for the entire room, I did a rapid calculation in my head. Was the potential for sex worth the cost?

Sure, why not? It would be an adventure, and I could always leave if he turned out to be a jerk.

I agreed, and we decided to meet in an hour.

Honestly, by the time I arrived, I was already wet at the thought of fucking a stranger.

We agreed to meet at the bar. If I didn't like what I saw, then I could just go home and call it a night.

After the idiots who preceded him, he was a pleasant surprise. Good-looking, slightly taller than my husband had been, probably about six-foot. His hair was neat, graying at the temples and silver streaked through his close-cropped beard. He looked fit even though he had a bit of softness above his belt. He was dressed casually in a light jacket, button-down shirt, and cotton pants. His shoes were casual lace-ups and thank God he wore socks. The whole sockless thing grossed me out.

I recognized him immediately from his picture. He stood and smiled as I approached, immediately offering to buy me a drink.

From where we sat at the bar, I could easily watch the bartender make my drink without worrying about something being slipped into it. It might have been years since I had dated, but I wasn't stupid.

We sat at the bar and chatted for about twenty minutes before he asked. "Well, what do you think? Do you feel comfortable enough to go upstairs with me?"

I smiled and nodded, quite proud of my bravery, and said, "Yes."

We walked over to the front desk clerk and rented a room. I was almost shocked when he put down his credit card and didn't ask me to pay half. From everything I'd heard, it hadn't occurred to me he'd pay for the entire thing.

The ever-vigilant part of me was glad that he didn't have a room booked already. It eased my trepidation about his expectations and his ability to plan ahead to do something vile to me. So far, everything seemed like it was going to be okay.

We went into the room, and he shrugged off his jacket before he helped me take off my coat and hung them both in the closet.

He came back to stand in front of me and put his hands on my hips. "Are you sure you want to do this?" he asked. "You can go home at any time. There's no pressure."

I really appreciated his consideration, but I'd been aroused before I got to the hotel. At this point, everything about him made me want to jump his bones. I stepped closer into his embrace and wrapped my arms around his shoulders.

"I'm okay with this." I assured him. "In fact, I've been wet since I left my house."

His relief was palpable. "Whew." He chuckled. "I've been hard since you walked in." He leaned in and brushed my lips gently and then brought one hand up to cup my cheek and thread his fingers through the hair at the nape of my neck, pulling me in closer to intensify the kiss.

It didn't take long for kissing to be not enough for me. I pressed myself against him, pushing my hips into his and rubbing up against the hard length of his cock between us.

"I think we need to shed some of these clothes," I said, proud of myself because I usually wasn't one to lead the way, but tonight I felt bold.

I stepped back from him and crossed my hands over my stomach and lifted the hem to take off my light sweater and reveal my lacy bra that did nothing to support my breasts, but damn they looked good in it.

He practically tore the buttons from his shirt as he took it off and then ripped his T-shirt off over his head. When he caught sight of my lace-covered breasts, he stuttered to a stop and stared.

I knew what he saw because I worried about my image in the mirror as I was getting ready. My dark nipples stood out through the creamy lace of my bra. I wasn't skinny, but I'd kept mostly in shape. Just a little soft around the edges.

"Damn, you are a fine-looking woman," he said as his hands cupped and molded me, testing my firmness, while his thumbs circled my peaks through the lace. "God, I love your tits." He undid the front latch on my bra.

Part of me wanted to be self-conscious, and the rest of me told it to go away. Sure, I wasn't twenty anymore, but he didn't seem to mind. I brought my hands to his shoulders, trailed my fingertips along his biceps and then smoothed my palms over his pecs, then his waist until I could reach the fastening of his pants. In seconds, I pushed them and his underwear down over his hips.

I had no idea where my bravery was coming from and didn't really care. His cock sprang free, jutting out like a spear between us, and oh my God, it was gorgeous.

My husband had been long and slender. While not a pencil dick, he had definitely been more length than girth.

This guy was above average in length and almost as broad as my wrist. The sight of him made my mouth water.

I couldn't wait to get him inside me. I took a step back and knelt down on my knees. I stuck my tongue out to taste the precious drop of pre-cum from his tip and smiled. Fuck, I'd missed the taste. Without hesitation, I took his head in my mouth and swallowed him as far as I could.

The sound of his quick intake of breath filled the room. He was so thick. I couldn't get very far along his length.

I did the best I could though. Sliding my tongue over his ridge and teasing that spot on the underside that used to make my husband vibrate.

His thighs tensed as my hand moved over his hip to grip his ass, holding him in place so he couldn't ease out of my mouth. My other hand slid up between his legs and played with his balls. Cupping their roundness as I kissed down his length, and I pulled them one at a time into my mouth. My tongue never stopped exploring him.

Still on my knees, I swallowed him again, hollowing out my cheeks to create a suction that, if his sounds above were any indication as he braced himself against the wall, he liked it. Very much.

"Jesus H. Christ." He tilted his head toward the ceiling as I peeked up at him through my lashes. "You give fantastic head."

I smiled and brought my hand around front again to jerk him off while I continued to gently stroke his balls. I kept my lips around his tip and slid my tongue over his slit until he pulled away.

"I'm going to cum if you keep doing that." He chuckled. "It'll be over before we even begin, and you don't even have your clothes off yet."

He reached out his hand and helped me to my feet as I kicked off my shoes and then hooked my thumbs into the waistband of my leggings and underwear and let them fall to the floor.

His hands were back on my waist as soon as I stood again. They drifted over my hips and reached around to hold my ass as he pulled me toward him. His cock poked me before it slid to the side, leaving a trail of pre-cum across my stomach in its wake as he held me against him. He looked down at my tits squished against his chest.

I followed his gaze, loving the way the hardness of his chest teased my peaks. The friction was delightful as I rubbed against him.

"Let's get you on the bed." He backed me toward the mattress while he looked over my shoulder to make sure I didn't misstep.

When the mattress hit the back of my knees, he put his hands on my elbows to help guide me down to a seated position and then told me to lie back.

I started to move over to the center, but he stopped me.

"No." He put his hands on my knees. "Stay on the edge of the bed." He pulled my legs slightly to position me to his liking. "I want your ass hanging off the edge."

Curious, I did as he requested, my feet on the floor, my legs spread, my pussy open to his gaze.

He put his hands on the mattress on either side of me and bent over, taking extra care to brush his chest across mine as he moved, purposefully letting me feel that exquisite sensation. Then he kissed me.

His lips were warm and firm against mine. His tongue explored with sure strokes. It was the only contact with my body except for the tip of his heavy cock as he hovered above me.

He left my mouth and whispered as he drifted toward my ear. "You are so beautiful." He nibbled on my lobe for a few seconds, and I could feel the empty ache increase between my legs.

"You feel so good against me." The anticipation was killing me. If he was this good already, I had high hopes for the rest of his performance.

He let his chest trail down over my stomach as his lips moved between my breasts. He sampled both with long kisses that suctioned each peak into his mouth before continuing his path over my stomach.

God, I was already addicted to the feel of him. My hands wove through his hair. It was thick with just a slight curl at the top. I ran my nails over the shorn sides and down over his neck and the top of his spine.

"Fuck, that feels good," he said with a growl that was so low it sounded like a purr. He rose again and nuzzled his face between my breasts to let me play a little bit longer before moving down until his shoulders nudged apart my thighs even further.

I heard a thunk as his knees hit the carpet. Then his hands drifted up my inner thighs until they were stroking my outer lips. I was soaked and could feel myself getting wetter as his thumbs picked up my slickness. The sensations as his digits moved up and down my puffy flesh before he bent them slightly to tease at the entrance to my channel and open me up wide.

I felt moisture drip down over my skin. I was almost embarrassed at how wet I was.

He definitely knew how to build up my anticipation.

I sighed with contentment.

"You like?"

My cheeks stretched into a grin. "I like. Very much. This is absolutely wonderful."

"Good to hear." His breath tickled across my wetness. "I'm just getting started." He took a long lick between my lower lips and ran the tip of his tongue over my clit.

I gasped when he hit that tiny bundle of nerves.

He just chuckled and did it again.

I closed my eyes, reveling in the feel of his mouth against me, amazed at how I felt so comfortable despite being with a stranger. I found my body moving in the same familiar rhythm that I always had with my husband when I realized that he was doing the exact same pattern my husband used to build my orgasm.

My entire body jerked in shock.

I sat up quickly and looked down at his confused face. Half expecting to see my late-husband's brown eyes staring up at me instead of my current lover's blue ones.

"Are you all right?" He started to get up, and I stopped him.

"No." My voice was too loud, even to my own ears. "No, everything's fine." I wasn't sure how to explain my reaction to him. "I guess we can call this a flashback. You just did something exactly like my husband used to. It freaked me out, but it was really nice too."

Understanding shone from his eyes. "Memories are powerful things."

"It just shocked me for a moment." I smiled. "I'm sorry. I didn't mean to make it weird."

He gazed at me for a second more to make sure I was really comfortable before he attempted to continue. "It's not weird. There are certain things that most of us guys, or at least those of us that care about pleasing a woman, have figured out. I'm glad I mimicked one of his good actions."

I nodded. "One of his best." I smiled and laid back on the mattress. "Sorry for the interruption, please continue." I waved my hand in the air as if I was the queen, telling her servant to carry on.

He chuckled and then went back to work. Picking up where he left off.

Now that my good memories blended with my current reality, it didn't take him long to make me start riding his mouth like a cowboy as he expertly read my body. He adjusted his pace when my thighs tightened around his ears. He didn't stop. He just let me take from him what I needed until I was exploding around him.

With my chest heaving, I relaxed back against the mattress as he continued to lap me gently with his tongue.

He lifted his head and smiled. His face was shiny with my juices. "You're so wet. If I fucked you now, you wouldn't feel me. I'll finish cleaning you off." He took a few exaggerated licks before he reached down to his pants and pulled the condom out of his front pocket.

"Are you okay if we continue?" he asked, holding up the foil disk.

Even after my flashback to Charles, I was fine. Any trepidation I'd had about having sex again flew out the window ages ago.

"Hang on a second." I sat up, legs still over the edge of the bed and motioned for him to come closer. "Before you wrap it up, I want another taste." I reached out and pulled his cock toward me. I engulfed his head with my lips, swirling the pre-cum over the tip with my tongue, before I swallowed him as far as I could. I gripped the rest of him in my hand to make up the difference.

He may not have been as long as my husband, but his girth made it harder for me to get very far down the shaft. I was determined to try. It was a new challenge. One I was ultimately destined to fail because he was just too damn big. But I liked it, and so did he, judging by the way his knees trembled.

It didn't take him long to back away again and say, "Seriously you are far too good at that." He motioned for me to get further up on the bed so he could join me.

I shifted on the mattress, and he came up between my legs on his knees.

One hand on my hips, the other on his cock, he positioned himself at the apex of my thighs and pressed in slowly.

I was glad I was still soaking wet. I needed every bit of lubrication as I stretched out around him. It had been almost a year since anything besides a silicone toy had entered me. He was so big. I felt every nerve ending as he stroked it on the way in and again as he pulled out.

It took him three tries before he reached the hilt. "God, you're so tight."

"Revirginization." I joked before gasping as he pushed in quicker this time. "Oh, you feel so good." I bent my knees and pushed my heels into the mattress to get a better angle.

He shifted to support my weight while he thrust in again. "Fuck." He groaned as his abs flexed with every motion. They may not have been defined anymore, but they were still sexy enough for me to enjoy watching as he plunged into me.

I reached up and stroked my hand over his chest as he leaned over me for a kiss.

As predicted, it didn't take long. I felt myself tightening again underneath him. The broad head of his cock hit me in places that hadn't been touched in a long time. Even my thickest vibrator couldn't compete.

"Are you almost ready? I don't think I can hold off much more," he gasped, the muscles in his biceps tense and the vein along his neck bulged out with his exertion.

I rose up and ground against him, doing a little circle with my hips to give me the pressure I needed to get off.

Understanding my need, he balanced on one arm and put his thumb between us. That was exactly what I needed to detonate. From this angle, I could feel my inner muscles clenching around him emphasizing the feel of that ridge as it slammed into my body. I felt the muscles in his legs clench between my thighs.

He gave out a guttural growl and another as he came inside me. Filling the condom before he collapsed, catching his weight on his elbows, to give me a series of slow kisses as we caught our breath.

I relished the weight of him over me. After all, human touch was what I was desperately missing. Having someone else pressed up against me.

Hell, even a cuddle or a hug would have satisfied me tonight for my first foray out, but what we shared had been exquisite. It was exactly what I needed.

He rolled away from me and said, "When you're ready, you can use the washroom first." His voice was wry. "I think I need a nap. You wore this old guy out."

"That's what my husband used to say." I laughed and glanced over at him.

There must have been a weird shadow because this time, I swore I was staring into my husband's brown eyes instead of my lover's blue ones.

My breath caught for just a moment, then I hastily gathered my things and padded into the bathroom. Once there, I stared at my reflection in the mirror, asking myself if I had completely gone insane. My hands shook as I got dressed.

As we left the hotel room, he asked if we could stay in touch.

While he seemed eager for a repeat performance, I was a little more hesitant. It was good. Very good. But I didn't want to jump into another relationship, and I knew I'd be tempted because he was easy to be with. I also knew I'd always be looking for a glimpse of my late husband again. Even if it had been a trick of the light.

I nodded and agreed with the caveat I'm not ready for anything serious yet.

He looked disappointed, but he understood. "Let me know when you're ready," he said. "The pickings aren't great at our age, but you are spectacular. You may have ruined me for anyone else."

I smiled at his cheesy line, gave him a half-hug and then walked out to my car.

Once I got home, I didn't bother to turn on the television. I sat in my darkened living room, had a glass of wine as I contemplated the evening's events.

I was proud of myself for getting out there and taking what I needed, but I was a little concerned about the flashbacks of my husband. Eventually, I decided it was probably natural to remember my husband during my first attempt at sex and eventually climbed up the stairs and went to bed.

It was another two weeks before I opened the hookup app again. I ignored the messages waiting from the previous guy. He was tempting, but I didn't want to fall into a relationship because it was easier than being alone.

I wanted to see what was out there before I risked getting involved with somebody else, even if it was just for sex.

Just like last time, my inbox was dinging like crazy with notifications. Within the first fifteen minutes of logging in, I received three separate dick pics and a dozen messages before one came in that wasn't completely crude.

From the looks of his picture, he was considerably younger than me. Unlike the others, he seemed polite and respectful, despite asking me if I wanted to have a young buck to satisfy me.

I reminded myself I was doing this to get out of my comfort zone and have an adventure. His approach was kind of funny, so I agreed to meet him.

I almost backed out when he warned me he was living in his mother's basement. I double-checked his age, thirty-two, and hesitated. My son was twenty-six, and he'd been out of the house for years. Was this guy some sort of weird mama's boy?

He must have been used to the reaction because he almost immediately assured me that he had a real job and paid his mom monthly rent. His dad had died a few years before, and he moved back in with his mom to help her out with the house. He lived in a small apartment downstairs in the basement and had a separate entrance.

When I pulled up to the house, I saw that it was very well maintained, and I recognized the truck he described in the driveway, complete with the construction company logo where he worked. I'll admit that eased my mind. I'd looked up the name of the company, and it turns out I knew a couple of people who work for them. The same guy who was in his profile photo was in several of the company's group shots. As long as he was the same guy, we were golden.

I had just exited my car when he came around the side. He looked younger than his picture. I had still half expected to have been catfished by some fat older guy who was still living in his mother's basement. But this fellow seemed to be who he'd claimed.

As we walked to his private entrance that led directly into his basement apartment, he pointed out different things he'd done for his mother over the years. He'd built her a small gazebo in the back and raised gardens along the front. This kid really seemed like he had it all together. Even though he wasn't much older than my son.

Something that I should probably feel ashamed of but couldn't bring myself to be.

Once we were down in the basement, he offered me a drink. When I declined, his grin got wide. "Are you ready to play then?" He grew serious for a moment. "We can stop if you get uncomfortable. I'm only having fun if you are."

I felt lucky that I happened upon two guys who had consent ingrained in them.

I looked him up and down and loved what I saw. His blonde hair was a little long but freshly washed, as if he had hopped in the shower after we arranged to meet. He was wearing a snug T-shirt with his company logo on the chest and a pair of grey sweatpants. Unlike the last guy, he had a six-pack, and it was very well-defined, even with his shirt on. When he turned to put the beer he'd been drinking on the counter, let's just say his ass did those sweatpants proud.

When he turned back toward me he was fully erect and the pants that were loose a moment ago were pulled taut across his hips as his dick extended out to greet me.

"You are even sexier in person." He wrapped his arms around me, bent his legs and shifted in one smooth motion until he lifted me off the floor and carried me down a short hall.

Stunned, I wrapped my legs around him and held on to him for dear life.

He just chuckled at my reaction, and I swear, his cock grew harder as he stepped into his bedroom. He tossed me gently on the bed and followed me down.

He moved one of his hands up under my shirt and began toying with my breasts.

I hadn't bothered with a bra tonight. I wore a hoodie and leggings.

His knees supported his weight between my legs, yet he still managed to press his cock right where I needed him. The sheer bulk of him promised all kinds of good things to come. His kiss wasn't tender or exploratory. He mashed our lips together in what should have been an assault, but I was already so turned on I just leaned up into him and rubbed my chest against his. Proud that my girls were still pretty firm despite my age.

"Fuck, I love your tits." He raised himself up to push up my hoodie. He bent his body, lifting his hips away from me, making me miss his weight as he bent down to suck hard on my nipples.

It was almost painful, yet I was soaked through my pants. Who could have known I'd like it rough?

He stood and stripped off my leggings, and suddenly I was naked from the top of my chest down. My hoodie remained bunched up under my armpits.

"I can't wait to fuck you," he said without finesse, which shouldn't have surprised me. I did find him on a hookup site.

As he tore off his gym pants, he hesitated. An almost imperceptible jerk shuddered his body, and without lifting his eyes to mine, he dove between my legs with his mouth.

I swear that hadn't been his plan thirty-seconds ago.

His big hands cupped my ass and pulled me close toward him. Then he started at my entrance and took a long lick up through my lower lips right up over my clit. I gasped when he hit that tiny bundle of nerves.

He just chuckled and did it again, moving in the same familiar rhythm identical to my husband's favourite manoeuvre.

What the actual fuck was happening? I wanted to pull away and get away from him, but his grip tightened.

He raised his head and said, "It's okay, Babe. I've got you." and I swear it was my husband's voice.

He dove back in, and my body reacted as if he were my husband while my mind grappled with impossibilities.

I dug in my heels and pushed myself up into his mouth without consciously deciding to enjoy the fantasy.

The shock that had shot through my body made me extra sensitive, and it didn't take long until I was pressing my clit against him as he worked. It didn't matter if it was his nose, chin, or lips. I needed that pressure from him, and he responded the way he always did, letting me use him for my own pleasure.

The tension built until it exploded. White light flashed behind my eyelids as waves of intense pleasure shattered me. When my trembling stopped, he moved up to cover my body, keeping his face in the shadow. Not giving me the opportunity to confirm or deny my delusion.

He plunged into me with one smooth stroke. He wasn't as wide as the fellow last time, but he made-up for it with hip action. He didn't just go in and out. He swiveled his hips, adjusting his angle and then flexing while he was deep inside my channel. It felt like he hit every nerve ending that existed in my body with each thrust.

I felt his ridge slide against my walls, as they expanded and tightened around him. It was exquisite torture that I never wanted to stop.

He grabbed my ankles and raised my feet up over his shoulders, pushing them slightly to raise my ass off the bed, then plunged into me harder, leaning his weight into my body. This new angle changed his trajectory. Everything hit differently as he plundered my depths. His head rubbed against my spongy flesh until I whisper-screamed at him to keep going.

He didn't stop. He picked up the pace just slightly and spread my legs wider to increase the friction even more.

Our breaths came in gasps.

"Cum for me, baby." His familiar words still in my husband's voice, and my body clenched obediently around him.

"Oh, fuck," he screamed as he convulsed inside of me.

I could feel every pulse as his orgasm jettisoned through him into me.

In that moment, I realized we'd forgotten to use a condom.

As soon as I had the thought, my husband's voice whispered through my mind. "It's all right. He's clean. I made sure of it."

When he rose from the bed, I was almost startled to see the young man's face again. He gave me a perfunctory kiss on the lips and said, "Well, that was fun. Do you wanna hang out for a few and we can do it again?"

I realized he hadn't even taken his shirt off, as he pulled his sweats back up his legs.

I smiled at the invitation. "No. Thank you, though." I gestured to my half-naked body and pulled my hoodie down over my breasts from where it had remained tucked into my armpits. "These old bones need to rest after that." I stood up from the bed to find where he had tossed my leggings. I found them in a pile of folded clothes in the corner.

Well, he was only thirty-two, but still. I rolled my eyes.

He followed me out to the kitchen and leaned against the counter while taking another pull from his beer as I slipped on my shoes. "If you ever want to get together again, hit me up. I love older women." He gestured to his cock, which was already half hard again.

"I see," I said, smiling because I knew that would never happen and let myself out of his apartment. Fervently hoping I wouldn't meet his mother along the way.

Once in my car, I took a deep breath and wondered what the hell was happening. Why was I hearing my husband's voice in the middle of having sex? Why did it feel like it was his mouth going down on me?

I was torn between freaking out and wanting to hook up with someone else to experiment.

Over the next few days, I went back on the app a few times. Just looking. I didn't swipe on anybody or respond to any messages. I don't even know what I was looking for, I just browsed.

Then, I saw him. He was a little younger than me, but at a quick glance, my husband's face stared up at me from my phone's display.

I blinked and looked back, and the guy really didn't look like Charles, yet he did. I didn't have the words to explain it other than my husband's face seemed to superimpose itself over the profile photo. Like one of those 3D vinyl stickers we could get when we were kids. A flower when you tilted it one way and a kitten when you tilted it the other way.

Was my husband choosing my next fuck for me? Was he going to channel through this guy? Is that what was happening? Or was grief over his loss causing me to lose my mind?

Before I could think twice, I swiped to show I was interested. When I didn't get an immediate response, I looked at the clock and laughed at myself. It was midmorning on a Wednesday. If this guy worked, he was probably not haunting the hookup app. I likely wouldn't hear from him for a few hours. It didn't matter if he didn't work. I didn't need his resume. He was just a hookup.

Happily, it didn't take long before he messaged me. He typed in full sentences. The usual getting to know you stuff not typically found on a site like this and no dick pic.

We sent a few messages back and forth over the afternoon and agreed to meet up that night after his last meeting ended around six.

I don't know why, but I gave him my address. I knew it was foolish and potentially unsafe. Maybe I was delusional, but it just felt like the right thing to do. I spent the rest of the afternoon getting ready, the same as I would have for a date with my husband. Since I was staying in, I wore a simple shift dress with nothing underneath.

He arrived promptly at six-thirty, coming directly from his meeting. In his hand he held a bouquet of brightly coloured Gerbera daisies.

My favourite flowers, even though he had no way of knowing. They were the ones my husband always brought me, and honestly, I didn't know whether to laugh or cry.

His shoulders seemed to sag in relief when he stepped into my home.

I resisted the temptation to question his reaction and put the flowers in water before I took him by the hand and led him upstairs to the bedroom. I wanted the fantasy. I didn't want to waste time getting to know him.

He'd taken his suit jacket off downstairs and ditched his tie. The rest of his clothes came off as soon as he walked into my bedroom. They dropped to his feet without a second thought.

Then he stepped towards me and wrapped his arms around me without taking my dress off. His embrace felt so familiar as he turned me toward the full-length mirror in the corner. He leaned in and whispered in my ear.

"It's good to be back."

I looked at our reflection, and I saw my husband's eyes looking at me the way he used to. I closed my eyes before turning toward the man who held me and let him kiss me the same way Charles had a thousand times before.

His hands bunched the fabric over my hips and then lifted it over my head. He turned me back to the mirror and pressed himself against my back. His long cock poked into my lower back. He nuzzled into the space between my neck and shoulder, using his big hands to cup my breasts. Pinching my nipples, slightly pulling them away from my body and then letting them plop back. His hands drifted down over my stomach, then lower, between my thighs in a well-practiced move.

I watched him in the mirror, marvelling as his hands shifted from the stranger's pale fingers to my husband's darker ones, until the pale ones ceased to exist altogether.

When the man lifted his head and joined my gaze in the mirror, my husband smiled back at me.

THE PRESENCE

Julie, my wife of a week, and I officially moved into our house yesterday.

We took possession the day before our wedding, and while we were away on our honeymoon, our extended family helped us by moving our furniture and the million-and-a-half boxes from our old apartment to our new home.

It was our dream house with three bedrooms, two and a half baths and a yard big enough to put a swing set and small above ground pool in eventually. It had an open floor plan for the kitchen, dining room and sunken living room.

The backyard was bordered by tall hedges on both sides and across the back, giving us privacy.

We'd fallen in love with the house at first sight and could easily picture starting our family here.

When we got back from our honeymoon, we discovered our moms had already unpacked our coffee maker and dishes. They'd also stocked our fridge with enough food to get us through the first few days until we could make a proper grocery run.

We stood in our kitchen that first morning, surrounded by boxes and our stuff in complete disarray. I wrapped her in my arms as we swayed slowly, gazing around our new home.

"We did it," she said, her eyes shining. "Married with a house before we turned thirty."

"Yes, we did." I pulled her closer. "We crushed it."

When we met on a dating app five years ago, that was part of my profile to let women know I was serious about finding a relationship. I wanted to be married and have a house by the time I was thirty. Julie's birthday was next month, and mine was two months after that.

Everything was perfect that first week as we unpacked. We'd both been able to take three weeks off from our respective jobs for our wedding, honeymoon and the move. By the time we had to go back to work, the only boxes left were Christmas decorations on the shelf in the garage.

My wife worked from home most days. After the pandemic, her office found it was more efficient to have staff work remotely.

I was a project manager for a construction company, and honestly, we found the house just in the nick of time as the high-rise complex our company was hired to build was just starting to ramp-up. It was going to require me to work a lot of overtime hours over the next few months. I would have hated leaving her to manage the entire move when I was at the office so much.

Not that she couldn't handle it herself. She was amazing. Still, she deserved a partner, not one of those alpha-bro males that beat their chests and did nothing else.

After my second day back at work, my wife was quieter than usual. We were relaxing in front of the TV after supper when she jolted and stared at the kitchen.

"What's the matter?" I asked.

"Nothing." Her voice was hesitant. "It's just…" She paused. "I've had this feeling most of the day. Like I'm being watched."

I started to get up to look around, and she stopped me.

"I've already checked." She gestured around the room. "Hell, I've even gone over the moldings to see if there were hidden cameras."

I glanced at the windows that looked into the backyard. It was dark beyond the deck's railing. No way to see if someone was outside looking in at us. "Maybe we should set up security cameras to be safe, since you're here alone all day."

"It doesn't feel like it's outside." Her voice was quiet. "Sometimes it feels like someone is standing beside me, even though no one is there."

I have to admit, her statement caused the hair on my arms to rise and a chill ran up my spine.

"I know I'm just being silly." Her smile was wry.

I pulled her toward me and held her close. "We've been so busy over the past few weeks with the wedding and the move. It's going to take a while to get used to the new house. It's a lot different from the condo, with different sounds and new neighbours. Don't discount your feelings."

"Thanks, babe." She hugged me back.

Later, as we undressed and crawled into bed, I leaned over to kiss her, and she clung a little harder to me. Her response seemed a bit desperate as if she still needed some reassurance. Which I gladly gave.

I held her gaze as I covered her body. Reaching down, I was surprised to feel how wet she already was for me.

Admittedly, it had been a few days since we'd done more than cuddle as we fell asleep. We'd both been too exhausted. We might be newlyweds, but we'd also been living together for almost four years. We were way past the incessant-sex phase and sleep often took priority.

Maybe the thought of someone watching turned her on. Although I doubted it, she didn't even like scary movies. She'd always made me change the channel if one came on.

Nevertheless, her wish was my command.

I kissed my way down her body, paying attention to each breast as I passed by, licking around the raised nubs before sucking on them gently.

Julie moaned as if her breasts were extra sensitive.

My heart stuttered. We started actively trying for a baby last month. Could she be pregnant already? I kissed over the smooth skin of her stomach as she bent her legs, raising her knees to build a tent of blankets over me as I kissed my way down between her legs.

She was so wet, and I took full advantage. I loved the way she tasted. Just the scent of her gave my cock a raging hard on which completely erased any vestiges of sleepiness I might have had when I crawled into bed beside her.

She tugged my hair. "Jason, I need you now."

I resisted. Even though she was ready, I didn't want her to miss out on an orgasm because I was too eager. I shifted my body weight down onto my haunches and dove in deeper. I tunnelled my tongue to reach further inside her entrance before easing back. I tilted my head enough to encircle her clit with my lips and alternate sucking and flicking her nub, while I used one finger, and then two, to press inside her channel.

I scissored them back and forth for a moment before curling them forward toward that spongy bit of tissue that made her back arch. Her cries were nearly muffled by the blankets over my head and the squeeze of her thighs over my ears.

I didn't stop. I wanted to keep her on the brink for as long as I could to ensure she'd sleep soundly when we were done.

Julie's hands grew frantic, pulling at my hair to get me to cover her and thrust myself inside her tight cunt. Now that she was ready, I pulled myself up and pressed my near-bursting cock where we both needed it.

Her sharp intake of breath at my intrusion was all the encouragement I needed.

Amelia Dax – Getting Ghosted Too

Her hands gripped my biceps and pulled me closer, urging me on. She wasn't normally so wild. Her grip, never this tight as she pressed herself against me. She rubbed her pelvis against my groin with every stroke.

This was going to be embarrassingly fast. I felt my body react to the way she clenched around my dick, which was a steel rod, as I responded to her passion.

I felt the telltale tingle at the base of my balls. My glutes tightened each time I hammered into her. Trying to slow down to make it last long enough for her to come again.

But she was having none of it. She urged me forward. "Harder. More."

Who was I to say no? I held still for an extra moment each time I plunged into her. Give her a chance to rub in small circles against me. Giving her the added stimulation she needed to finally detonate under my body. Her fingernails dug into my skin as I pounded into her one last time before I exploded.

The rush of pleasure took the last of the energy from my muscles, yet I hovered over her until she was still again.

Even though I was spent, I got up to pad into our ensuite bathroom. I ran the water until it was warm and dampened a washcloth to clean her up.

She sighed contentedly as I washed her lady bits and was asleep before I finished.

As I tossed the warm washcloth toward the hamper, I swear I saw a flash of movement in the chair over by the window. I squinted into the darkness. There was nothing there, no shadow or figure. I reached to turn on the bedside lamp to investigate, then hesitated because I didn't want to wake Julie up.

I stood and walked over to the chair to be sure.

Nothing. Just a lingering feeling of being watched.

It took me hours to relax enough to fall asleep.

The next morning everything seemed to be back to normal.

Julie looked well rested, and when I asked, she said, "I had the best night's sleep. Thank you." Her smile was genuine, and her touch lingered on my arm whenever she passed me the coffee or the cream.

I was still freaked out and reluctant to leave, knowing I wouldn't be home until late again tonight.

"Are you sure you're going to be okay here alone?" subtly referring to our conversation the night before.

She hesitated for a split-second before taking a breath. "I'll be fine. I just freaked myself out yesterday."

I debated telling her about what I thought I saw and decided against it. Instead, I vowed to pick up some interior cameras at lunch and install them when I got home. I needed to ensure she was safe and that the movement in our bedroom had just been a figment of my imagination.

I hated that I needed to be on the construction site all day today. It was half an hour further away from our house than my office.

She was at the counter when I gathered my things to leave. I held her close and kissed her. "I'm just a phone call away if you need me. Call me for anything."

"I know, Babe," she reassured me. "I'll be fine. If I get uncomfortable, I can head down the street to that cute little café and work from there."

Her solution offered me only a little relief.

Still concerned, I walked out to my car, absently rubbing the sore spot her fingers scratched into my bicep. That memory wasn't scary. It brought a smile to my face because she'd never been that wild in bed before.

At the worksite office trailer, the day stretched on. I was constantly distracted with worry about my wife. Every moment dragged as I coordinated details with the foreman and his team. I resisted the urge to call her every hour on the hour.

Thankfully, she took pity on me and texted me throughout the day to let me know she was fine and had decided it was just her imagination getting the better of her in the new surroundings.

I still stepped out at lunch to buy the security cameras.

As soon as I could, I rushed home and walked in the front door to the dissipating smell of dinner. Sure enough, there was a pan soaking in the sink and a covered plate in the refrigerator for me. I'd warned her I was going to be later than planned and was glad she didn't wait for me to eat.

I popped the leftovers into the microwave. Then made my way down to her office, assuming she was still working, when I heard a gasp from the bedroom.

Four strides later, I stood in the doorway with a smile as I saw my wife naked on the bed, legs spread, angled toward me. I stripped off my dusty work shirt, relieved she wasn't upset because of my unexpected delay tonight, when I realized she wasn't pleasuring herself.

She lay spread-eagled on the bed. Her arms extended, and her hands gripped the sheets in tight fists.

It was then I noticed her breasts moving of their own accord. Indentations undulated over her flesh as if an invisible hand was cupping and kneading her chest. Her nipples stood erect, their peaks stretched up, twisting slightly, as if some unseen hand was plucking them.

Like last night, she dug her heels into the mattress as her hips thrust upward as if she was fucking someone.

There was no one on the bed with her.

I collapsed against the doorway. Fear warred with disbelief. From my vantage point, I could see the edges of her entrance shifting back and forth as if something was pushing against her flesh and then pulling out.

I stepped into the room to rescue her from… from what I had no idea.

She gasped and arched up, pressing herself toward whatever was moving against her clit.

There was nothing. Nobody was there, but I watched her labia part and move in response. Indents appeared at her hips, and she flipped onto all fours as if someone had grabbed her by the waist and repositioned her.

She wasn't a big woman but there was no way in hell I could have managed that move so easily.

Her knees were nudged open wider, and an imprint on her back encouraged her to tilt her ass up as she stayed on all fours.

Unseen hands caressed her ass cheeks, and then her arms were guided out straight until she'd bent forward onto her elbows.

Her tits brushed the mattress until they didn't. They were held up and moved on their own as if being massaged. Her nipples reddened as unseen fingers rolled them back and forth between them before they fell back against the bed.

What the actual fuck was going on? I stood frozen to the doorframe as something spread the cheeks of her ass wide and then repositioned her to ensure I had a straight-on view of her sopping pussy and the small rosebud, which in this position, pointed toward the ceiling.

In an instant, her puckered hole shone with moisture. She moaned as the tiny hole opened slightly as the flesh surrounding it seemed to move. Her moans got louder, and even more wetness appeared on her skin.

"Oh God, yes." She panted against the bedspread as the opening grew wider. The ring of muscle surrounding her anus moved slightly as if it was being manipulated. More wetness and the hole got bigger. Shifting back and forth as if there were two objects fighting for space.

Galvanized, I raced to my wife but hit a wall of warm solid flesh.

Naked flesh.

The impact knocked me back against the doorframe. Whatever stood between me and my wife was built like an oversized linebacker.

"No," I whispered in shock. "NO!" I screamed louder and ran toward her again. This time I felt a massive hand around my neck. My body rose until my feet cleared the floor, as I was shoved backward, nearly out the bedroom door.

No response except for Julie's shout. "Oh. My. Fuck." Her asshole now stretched out as something glided between her ass cheeks. A slap echoed through the bedroom as a pink handprint appeared on rounded flesh. Then, indents on her waist appeared again as the lower half of her body lifted from the bed and was shifted back and forth by whatever was cornhole-ing my wife.

"No," I sobbed and slid down to the floor. My head banged against the doorframe, knowing I couldn't stop what was happening.

"Yes!" she screamed as her body was lifted nearly upright and turned toward me.

She'd thrown her head back in ecstasy.

Eyes closed.

Breathless.

Her tits pushed up as if there was something underneath them, holding her up for display. Her legs were still spread, knees bent, feet braced on something between the soles to hold her in position as I watched her mound move back and forth as something massaged her clit and fingered her channel.

From my spot on the floor, I could see her ass cheeks rhythmically squish against something behind her.

Terrified, with tears streaming down my face, I watched my wife orgasm.

The tethers that held her shifted until she was carried bride style, and then she was placed gently on the bed.

I stood up and walked carefully toward her. Relieved that this time nothing blocked me. "Julie, Honey? Are you all right?"

My wife had settled against the bed with a smile on her face. At the sound of my voice, her eyes fluttered open.

"Hi Babe." She yawned. "I must have fallen asleep." She looked down at her naked body and laughed. "I was going to be sexy and wait for you in bed, but I couldn't keep my eyes open." She shifted to get up and grimaced. "Man, I'm sore. I must have worked out too hard this afternoon."

A blast of heat drifted by me, and I swear I heard a low rumble of laughter echoing faintly down the hallway.

Despite my wife's objections, we spent the night in a hotel and put the house up for sale the next day.

JUDY'S VENGEANCE

Author's Note:

Judy's Vengeance is a standalone short story, which is also a sequel to Judging Judy, published in the first Getting Ghosted book. The original story centered around the intelligent-looking statue of a fox wearing glasses in the bathroom of the Write Cup Bookstore Café.

Two weeks after the book was published, someone stole the statue. It was never seen again.

So of course, a sequel had to be written.

The same couple were here again. They've been in my bathroom almost every day for the last week and a half. Ever since Amelia read the erotic short story, she penned about me.

At first, I was a little embarrassed, and a lot honoured that Amelia seemed to be able to read my thoughts so easily and thought them worthy of publishing.

There was an unexpected side effect from the book... let's just say the frequency of people getting it on in my bathroom for me to watch, and dare I say judge, increased exponentially.

Seriously, I'm not being conceited. Well, at least not this time.

People spoke to me directly. Telling me they were coming into the bathroom just so I could watch them have sex.

Amelia made me a fucking tourist attraction.

I'd been stationed here for a few months before Amelia's book made me famous. After my initial hesitation, I loved my position here. Lording over the bathroom to judge all who went before me at the bookstore-café. They even had a nickname for me, Judging Judy. Yes, after the TV personality.

But I digress, back to this couple. They didn't seem to be the brightest bulbs on the tree, if you'll allow my unseasonal metaphor. Other couples certainly had more grace, more imagination. But the only strong point these two seemed to have was enthusiasm.

Her favourite position was to bend at the waist and put her hands on either side of the door frame so he could take her from behind. Her entire priority seemed to be to make sure that I could see everything he did.

Sure, I was flattered, but it seemed she was taking my perusal of their activities a little too seriously. She constantly made him adjust so I could get a better look.

This time it was when the poor guy was mid-ejaculation. He ended up jizzing on her back because she made him lose his balance.

I sighed as they cleaned up and left, and then I went on with my day. Judging people for the length of time they washed their hands and double judging if they didn't bother washing their hands at all.

Mid-afternoon, I had a guy bring one of Amelia's books from the front shelf into the bathroom and jerked himself off while he read my story aloud. Well, at least the good parts.

From the way his stallion rose tall at the mention of that tall cowboy with the great ass, he had a little country western in him.

After several strokes along his hefty girth, I imagined he'd become a fountain and was his own tall drink of water.

Oh, that was a good one. Amelia, quick, come read my mind.

Actually, it was sort of fun watching him stroke himself. I got a full view. There was no one else to get in the way.

The slickness of his pre-cum dripped over his knuckles as he read from the book in his other hand. He leaned so far back to give himself more room. I thought he was going to crack the toilet tank in the process. His cock had a really nice head. Broader than his shaft, it stopped his hand from flying off the end once he got going. His thumb rubbed the pre-cum over his tip without breaking his rhythm.

I was watching a master at work.

Then, I saw his balls pull up towards his body in that telltale sign that he was about to blow his load.

And he did.

All over the wall behind me. He narrowly missed the chain of my glasses.

Then, to my surprise, he took out a pencil and made tiny marks on the wall at the top of his cum-track.

Wait. Did they just make me into a competition? Had I become a goalpost? A personal record to surpass next time?

I was okay with it. It sounded like a great game. As long as the participants washed me off afterward.

As if reading my mind, he wiped down the wall, cleaned himself up and headed back out to the bookstore-café.

I really hoped he bought Amelia's book and didn't just put it back on the shelf. Ewww.

We were close to the end of the day when the young fellow from this morning came back. This time, without his girlfriend. He used the bathroom and then, without washing his hands, grabbed me.

"What the fuck is happening?"

I screamed as loud as I could. Since I was a plastic, brass-looking statue, my cries for help were silent.

He twisted me off the screw that held me to my perch, despite me begging for my life.

"What are you doing?" I yelled at the idiot whose rough hands were manhandling me into a backpack. "Put me back on the wall this instant."

The asshole, male, blonde, about five-foot ten with a pancake butt and the aforementioned lack of good sense to wash his hands, ignored me and zipped up the bag, plunging me into total darkness.

Then he had the nerve to crack me against the doorframe as he descended the two steps leading out to the main space.

"Help. Help! HELP!" I shrieked. Surely someone could sense that I was in peril as I bumped along, trapped in a bag, probably never to be seen again.

But no, I heard the bookstore-cafe's staff wish my abductor a good evening as he sauntered out of the shop.

He didn't seem to be in a hurry. I heard traffic, people, the annoying beep at crosswalks, and then the hum of air-conditioning and a store announcing its Wednesday special. Spicy Italian sausages on sale for twenty-five percent off. Wednesday?

No, this wasn't fair. My favourite sausage was going to be at the bookstore-café tonight. God bless him, he always washed his dick after he used the washroom, giving me a full-frontal view. I may be a guy, but I will always appreciate a good cock.

Maybe I could hop out of this idiot's bag when he tried to put his groceries in. Yes, I acknowledged, it would be easier if I had a body. Maybe someone will see me inside the bag, recognize me and take me home to the bookstore-café.

My hope was in vain. The bag I was stuffed in stayed on the moron's back while they carried their groceries in a reusable bag he'd had in an outer pocket of his knapsack.

So far, that was the only thing redeemable about this person. Even his groceries left a lot to be desired. At least

84

according to the self-checkout that confirmed each item: twelve-pack of bargain mac and cheese, a dozen wieners and a half-dozen beer.

Ding, ding, ding, we have a winner at adulting… not.

He hummed as he walked up the street, which really pissed me off.

Did he feel satisfaction and a feeling of accomplishment for stealing me off the wall?

Well, if he did, it wasn't going to last for long because I vowed I was going to make sure he never felt satisfied again as I bumped along with every step.

We went uphill and then down as the traffic sounds faded behind us, heading toward one of the less affluent parts of town.

My hopes for escape crashed and burned when I heard keys in a lock, footsteps on a wooden floor and the cans in the grocery bags thunk on a table. The knapsack I was trapped in got shrugged off his back and tossed onto a couch, or maybe a chair. Probably a futon that doubled as his bed.

"What the hell do you think you're doing?" I screamed at him. Knowing he couldn't hear me, but I desperately needed to find some way to connect with him, so he'd take me home.

I never thought I'd miss the bookstore-café but damn it, I did.

Without hearing me, he put away his groceries.

I heard the clunk of the beer cans as he pulled one out of those infernal plastic strips and felt the weight of him as he settled down beside me.

When he pulled me out of the backpack, he had a big smile on his face. He just stared at me as if I was the answer to his prayers.

I was going to be his worst nightmare if I could just figure out how.

Just then, a cheap, tinny sound echoed through his apartment.

He put his beer on the coffee table and eagerly got up to answer the door, hiding me behind his back as he opened it.

"Did you get it? Did you get Judy?" I recognized the female voice immediately. It was his girlfriend.

She pushed past him. "Where is it? Where is it? I've gotta see it."

For the love of all that's holy, he stole me to impress a girl. If I had a thought-bubble it would be filled with question marks and exclamation marks.

What the actual fuck?

She turned around and realized he held a hand behind his back. "Let me see. Let me see."

Seriously, couldn't this girl say anything without repeating it?

He pulled it out and handed it to her. Pride shining in his eyes as if he had won Olympic gold instead of foxy bronze.

"Oh my God, I can't wait to let her judge us, just like the author said she would."

"He would," the guy and I said at the same time. "Remember, she said he was a dude."

He tossed me onto the chair and wrapped his arms around her, but she beat him off.

"No. We gotta do it right," she said. She pushed him away, raced to the chair and then put me on the coffee table.

When I fell on my back and looked up at the ceiling, she grabbed the knapsack and put it on the coffee table behind me to lean on, so I was staring at the futon.

See, a futon. I called that one right, didn't I?

Now that I could see the apartment, it was exactly as I thought. Just a pissant little studio with a kitchen sink and hot plate in the corner. A doorway led off to what I assumed was the bathroom.

Truthfully, it could have gone either way. The number of fancy diamond rings and Italian leather loafers that had sex in my bathroom since the book came out made it just as possible that I could have been secreted out of town in an Audi or Lexus.

Meanwhile, my new mistress giggled and started ripping off her clothes. I guess I never thought of my voyeurism being able to make someone horny, so there you go. Learn something new every day.

He followed suit and was naked by the time he got on the futon.

She lay down with her legs spread in front of me, assuming I'd enjoy the view. Then she thought better of it and laid lengthwise.

"Why'd you move?"

"Your ass will get in the way, and then Judy can't see us."

If I could have rolled my eyes, I would have. If I ever get back to the bookstore, Amelia and I are going to have words. She's the one who put me in this position.

He glared at me, and I glared right back. "You really want it watching us."

"Of course, silly," she said. "That's the whole reason I got you to steal it. If we're good, maybe, we'll be in the next book."

This time, I wasn't the only one who thought she was nuts. Did she think I wrote the books? It almost gave me a modicum of sympathy for him. He was obviously wrapped around her little finger, but a crime is a crime, and he did it willingly.

I stared at him.

He stared at me.

I tried to narrow my eyes. It must have worked because I felt a zing pass between the two of us.

Then, the most incredible thing happened. His erect cock, which under any other circumstances would have been impressive, shrivelled. It didn't just deflate. It shrunk right down to almost prepubescent size.

Extraordinary.

He looked horrified.

She looked disappointed.

I laughed my ass off. Or I would have if I had one. Maybe I had some power after all.

Frantically, he started working at his nob, trying to get his erection back, while she sat there dumbfounded.

"Babe? What happened? Where'd it go?"

"I don't know. It just went away." He was practically crying as he beat his meat to no avail.

I snickered. This wasn't just great. It was awesome. I don't know if it was some power mysteriously bestowed on me or his own guilty conscience, but he was as flaccid as a wet noodle. Not even linguine, more like spaghettini.

"Suck me off." He was frantic. "Do something."

Obediently, she scooted forward on the futon, put her feet on the floor and grabbed his cock in her hand and stroked it a few times.

Nothing happened.

Desperately, she swallowed him. In a single motion, her lips kissed his balls, and I could see her tongue frantically working around his head, stroking his length while her fingers came underneath and cupped his balls. She even played with his tight, puckered hole, trying to get any reaction from him.

His cock remained deflated. Deader than a doornail. There was no getting it up.

"What happened?" she said as she took his cock out of her mouth. "I don't understand."

"I don't know. I was rockin' a hard-on and then I looked at that damn statue. I swear he narrowed his eyes at me and I went limp. Like all the feeling is gone. I'm numb." He glared at me again. "We've got to take it back. It's cursed. That thing can't stay in my house. I'll never get another boner if it stays here." He started to panic.

She laughed at first, but then she looked at his limp dick. "You've never had trouble getting it up with me before."

"I want to. Fuck. I want to. I stole it for you. I stole that fuckin' statue for you 'cause you wanted it. Now my dick's dead."

She stared at me, and then she looked at his limp cock and then back at me.

I could see the tennis ball bouncing back and forth in her head. "But that's silly. The statue can't make you go limp."

"The statue can't judge how good we do sex either," he said. "It's just a plastic statue."

"But the author…" she trailed off.

"The author told a story to sell books." His voice was gentle. "You know that, right? She just made up a story about the statue in the bathroom."

"If it's just a story about a statue, then why can't you get it up?"

"Maybe I feel guilty for stealing. Mama told me never to steal, that nothing good would come of it, and now I can't even come. That's not good."

"Okay," she grumbled. "Take it back."

He looked at his watch. "It's too late. They're closed now."

"Well, if you can't get it up, you better do something else." She spread her legs wide and put her fingers down to spread her lips, so he and I both had a full view. "Get busy, or I'm going out with the girls."

He dropped to his knees and began licking and sucking for all he was worth.

She leaned back and stared at the ceiling. Every few minutes, she'd give me a dirty look as if it was my fault I was ruining her sex life.

Well, I guess it was, but she's the one who told him to steal me. She started it.

She sighed. "It's not working." She closed her legs, nearly kicking him in the head as she rolled over to get up. She got dressed and walked to the door. "Since we can't have any fun, I'm going to go out with the girls. Let me know when you can get it up again."

With that, she exited, leaving him and me alone in the apartment.

His limp cock still flopping between his legs

"I'm sorry," he said to me, and I just glared at him. He turned on the TV, and I got to stare at him while he watched. He didn't even have the courtesy to turn me around so I could see the screen. Asshole.

An hour or so later, he picked me up and tossed me in the trash.

I silently screamed because it meant I wasn't going home to the bookstore-café. I heard him rustling around and then I started laughing as I heard him frantically trying to give himself a hand job and cursing at himself for not being able to get it up. I could only hope that by morning he'd realize he had to take me back, or he would never have sex again.

Eventually, he pulled me out of the trash and dropped me back on the coffee table. He crashed onto the futon, leaving me to breathe in the fumes from the rest of the six-pack he'd drained.

It was still a fifty-fifty crapshoot whether he was going to take me back or throw me out. Now that I was back on the coffee table, I was a little more hopeful.

The next morning we both awoke to banging on his apartment door. He groggily got up and scratched his balls on the way over.

His girlfriend burst in, nearly breaking his foot in the process. "The cafe opens in ten minutes. Why aren't you ready?" she screamed at him.

He scratched the back of his head. "I was getting to it."

She pushed him toward the bathroom. "Go get a shower and get dressed. We've gotta take it back."

"Okay, okay," he grumbled. "I don't know what the rush is."

I could hear the shower going while she paced the floor. Every once in a while, she stopped to stare at me.

"You're a real asshole, you know," she said.

I reeled back in shock. "Me? I'm the one who was abducted."

She turned to the bathroom to make sure the shower was still going. "I tried to hook up last night, and I couldn't. I couldn't get wet, and the guy went limp as soon as I touched him. His cock just died, just like." She pointed her thumb over her shoulder toward the bathroom. "You're bad luck. We gotta get rid of you."

She went to toss me in the trash when he came out of the bathroom.

"It doesn't work. I already tried to throw him out. We gotta take it back."

She nodded and then rinsed me under the tap because I was all sticky from where he'd spilled the beer on the coffee table.

Damn, that hot water felt good.

A few minutes later, I was shoved back into the backpack. I'm happy to say his pace was much faster on the way down to the bookstore-café. I was never so happy to hear familiar voices greeting customers. She stopped to get coffee, and he took me directly to the bathroom and hauled me out of his bag.

I looked around the familiar room and breathed a sigh of relief.

The owners had already put up a different sign to cover the screw in the wall where I'd originally hung. I had to laugh because the new sign said, "Get naked" and then underneath in smaller print, "Just joking, this is a 1/2 bath don't make it weird."

I loved it and would be sad to see it go. But I was here first.

He took the framed print down and reattached me to the wall. Not knowing what to do with the frame, he just sat it in the basket on top of the toilet tank where they kept the extra toilet paper.

There was a knock on the door.

He opened it, and she forced her way in. She had a huge grin on her face.

"I'm horny." She put the two coffee cups on the vanity and pointed to his pants. "Can you get it up now that the damn thing is back where it belongs?"

He and I both looked down at his crotch, and his sweatpants tented. We both breathed a sigh of relief.

She dropped her jeans, letting them pool around her ankles, and bent over the toilet, bracing her hands on the back of the seat. "Fuck me."

He had enough presence of mind to reach behind him and lock the door before pulling out his boner. He barely checked to see if she was wet before he plunged into her.

They both sighed in relief when he reached the hilt.

While I didn't have the best vantage point, I didn't care.

He thrust away, and they both made happy noises. It was over in about three minutes.

I don't think any of us complained. They had their sex life back, and I was home again and more than happy to see the end of them.

As the morning wore on, a couple of the before lunch-regulars came in. They didn't react to my being back, but since they hadn't been there since yesterday morning, they didn't know I'd been missing.

Then one of the staff members came in to do a cleanliness check, did a double take and hollered out into the main café area.

"Judy's back! They brought Judy back."

Suddenly there was a crowd of on-duty staff, the two owners and a couple of regulars staring in amazement at my shining countenance on the wall.

It felt good to be missed. Not that I planned on going on any more adventures.

The fates seemed to reward me for my patience.

Yes, I had three more couples in during the day as if wanting to make sure I had plenty to judge and would never leave again.

I still needed to have a chat with Amelia though. No more stories!

Amelia Dax – Getting Ghosted Too

AFTERWORD

If you enjoyed this story, please leave a review on Goodreads, Fable or your favourite book retailer.

Your reviews help more than you can imagine.

Stay Sexy,
Amelia

Amelia Dax – Getting Ghosted Too

OTHER BOOKS BY AMELIA DAX

Find them at your favourite retailer
https://linktr.ee/ameliadax

Earth Outpost 6-9

Nestled near the asteroid belt between Mars and Jupiter, Earth has 360 monitoring stations. Damian and Elin are stationed at Outpost 6-9. A coincidence? Perhaps not. They will do anything to make their interstellar guests feel welcome… ANYTHING.

Eventually, they learn their role isn't just fun and games. The universe is vast, humans are weak, and soon they'll need all the interstellar friends they can get.

Horni-Culture

What if that little house on the prairie had plants you could use as sex toys?

The world as we know it has ended. Those who are left, struggle to survive. Until they discover a mysterious species of plants that help them find a little joy and a lot of orgasms.

Amelia Dax – Getting Ghosted Too

Merry Elfin' Christmas

Two Christmas stories your mom definitely never read to you at bedtime. In Shelf-less Shenanigans, Herald, an Observer Elf, delivers an extra helping of Christmas Cheer to a divorced woman spending her first Christmas alone. Then we head to the North Pole for Reclaiming Mrs. Claus, where a few enthusiastic elves get Mrs. Claus all fired up to reclaim her family's legacy from a wayward Santa.

Getting Ghosted

Six sexy short stories about things that bump in the night. Sentient headphones with a voice so deep you can feel his touch. A ghost finally gets a piece of the action after haunting an apartment for decades. A hot hitchhiker who disappears into thin air, and three more unexplainable erotic encounters.

If you enjoy fun, sexy times, you'll love these short story series.

Get my complete book list at:

Amelia Dax – Getting Ghosted Too

AUTHOR BIO

Forgettable by day and incredible at night, Amelia Dax takes inspiration from the world around us and beyond. She crafts fun stories of lust and satisfaction.

@ameliadaxerotica

amelia@ameliadax.com

www.ingramcontent.com/pod-product-compliance
Lightning Source LLC
Chambersburg PA
CBHW020754130626
46554CB00006B/2174